DREAM WANDERERS
APPRENTICES

I0600908

PAULA BROWN

A Mouse Gate™ Adventure

Mouse Gate™
1103 Middlecreek
Friendswood, Texas 77546
281-992-3131 TEL
www.totalrecallpress.com

All rights reserved. Except as permitted under the United States Copyright Act of 1976, No part of this publication may be reproduced, stored in a retrieval system, or transmitted in any form or by any means electronic or mechanical or by photocopying, recording, or otherwise without prior permission of the publisher. Exclusive worldwide publication / distribution by TotalRecall Publications, Inc..

Copyright © 2016 by: Paula Brown
All rights reserved
ISBN: 978-1-59095-792-9
UPC: 6-43977-77992-2

Printed in the United States of America with simultaneous printings in Australia, Canada, and United Kingdom.

FIRST EDITION
1   2   3   4   5   6   7   8   9   10

Library of Congress Control Number: 2016948324

This is a work of fiction. The characters, names, events, views, and subject matter of this book are either the author's imagination or are used fictitiously. Any similarity or resemblance to any real people, real situations or actual events is purely coincidental and not intended to portray any person, place, or event in a false, disparaging or negative light.

The scanning, uploading and distribution of this book via the Internet or via any other means without the permission of the publisher is illegal and punishable by law. Please purchase only authorized electronic editions, and do not participate in or encourage electronic piracy of copyrighted materials. Your support of the author's rights is appreciated.

In loving memory of my
brother-in-law Steve Holzner.

Thank you for making
my sister so happy.

About the Author

Paula Brown is a freelance travel writer who also has a love for science fiction and Walt Disney World. Paula is the coauthor of *Dining at Walt Disney World: The Definitive Guide.* She is also a contributing author to *InsiderScoop®* to *Walt Disney World®* series of books. Other works of fiction include The *Coffee Cruiser* and *It's About Time.* Paula lives in Florida with her husband and daughter.

About the Book

Gren is excited because her little sister Winnie and Winnie's friend Mollie are going to spend their school break with her. Gren's friends Calli and Tayo agree to spend their break with her as well, to help take care of the children while Gren is at work. What Gren doesn't know is that Mollie has a problem that she wants assistance with; her dreams come true. Someone learns of Mollie's ability to see the future and sets a plan in motion to kidnap her and profit from her gift. What the person doesn't realize is that Winnie was grabbed instead. Gren and her friends use their skills to try to find Winnie, before the kidnapper realizes the mistake.

Prologue

"Now, Gren, are you sure you have everything? Magic Bands, sunscreen, money for lunch, hats, water bottles?"

"Yes, Mom. Winnie and I will be fine." Gren fingered a piece of paper in her pocket. "I have everything that we'll need."

"Cell phone?"

Winnie laughed. "Gren doesn't go anywhere without her cell phone these days."

"I don't know, maybe your father and I should go with you. Winnie is still so young..."

Gren took a deep breath and let it out slowly. "Mom, I'm going to be moving away soon because of my internship. I want to spend some quality time with my little sister. We've never done anything like this before. You need to stay here and take care of Dad. That's the worst sunburn that I've ever seen, you know that he needs you."

"You're right." The girls' mother hugged them both. "Call me at some point."

"We will, Mom." Gren took her sister's hand, mostly for show. "Come on, Winnie, let's get out front so we can catch the bus to Disney's Hollywood Studios."

⚬ ⚬ ◉ ◉ ⚬ ⚬

As soon as they were out the door Winnie let go of her sister's hand. "So do I get to meet him today?"

"Who?" Gren pretended that she didn't know what Winnie was talking about.

"Your boyfriend."

"He's not my boyfriend."

"Then why do you text him several hundred times a day?" Winnie teased.

"It's, well, it's complicated," Gen explained. "We met last time we were here, on Rock 'n' Roller Coaster. We hit it off really well. We felt like we had known each other forever, so we keep in touch. That's all." Gren knew very well that *wasn't* all, but she couldn't really explained her connection to Lawson and still sound sane. "But the answer to your question is yes, you will get to meet him today. He's going to meet us there."

"Why didn't you tell Mom about him?"

"Because Mom would jump to conclusions, just like you did. Now hurry up, we don't want to miss the bus."

∘ ∘ ◐ ● ◑ ∘ ∘

Half an hour later Gren and Winnie walked through the bag check line. Lawson was waiting for them on the other side. He and Gren smiled at each other for a moment, both remembering the last time that they had met. They then shared a hug. Gren heard Winnie whisper, "Boyfriend," as they embraced.

"Lawson," Gren said as they let go, "this is my little sister, Winnie."

"It's nice to finally meet you, Winnie. I've heard so much about you."

"In the several hundred texts that you send to my sister each day?"

"Yup."

Winnie looked Lawson up and down. "Lawson...as in Denis Lawson? The actor who played Wedge in *Star Wars*?"

Lawson laughed. "You two are definitely sisters. Gren is the only other person who ever figured that out."

"You seem nice enough. Let's go in."

As they passed through the front gate, Gren glanced at Mickey's of Hollywood. She had first seen Lawson in the store the previous year. That trip had changed her life forever.

"Feels like a long time ago, doesn't it?" Lawson commented.

"Yeah." Gren paused. "You bring yours?"

"Of course I did. Roy told us to hold onto them. We only have the two, though, so I'm not sure what we're going to do today."

"Who is Roy?" Winnie asked. "Never mind, I probably don't want to know. Shouldn't we be getting into line for Toy Story Midway Mania? It's almost our FastPass+ time."

"Okay, little sister, let's get going."

Winnie didn't move. "Wait. How is Lawson going to ride with us?"

Gren grinned. "I linked our accounts online. He has the same FastPass+ times that we have."

"So what are we waiting for?" Winnie asked. "Let's go ride!"

○ ○ ● ◉ ● ○ ○

The first part of the day the threesome had a lot of fun. After Toy Story they rode Star Tours twice, followed by the Great Movie Ride, and then they caught the first Beauty and the Beast show of the day. After the show ended Lawson pulled a piece of paper out of his pocket. "Looks like it's time," he said. "I just don't know how we're going to handle this. Maybe just you two go, I'll wait outside."

"That won't work," Gren protested. "We all need to ride."

"What are you talking about?" Winnie asked.

"I know, but we only have two magical FASTPASSES."

"What are you talking about?"

"Yeah, but..."

A female cast member with curly hair picked something up

in front of them. "Here, you dropped this." She handed Gren a piece of paper and quickly hurried away.

Gren looked at the paper and smiled at Lawson. "We now have three."

"WHAT ARE YOU TALKING ABOUT?"

"Little sister, how would you like to ride Rock 'n' Roller Coaster? It's the best ride here."

"I don't know...I've heard it's pretty intense."

"Intense is the perfect word for it," Lawson mumbled.

"You can handle it," Gren quickly added, hoping that Winnie had not heard Lawson's comment. "You loved Space Mountain."

"Yeah, but..."

"Fine. I'll tell Mom that you're not ready for the fun rides. Let's head over to Epcot and ride Gran Fiesta Tour. You can probably handle that one."

Winnie changed her strategy. "Isn't the line too long by now?"

"We have magical FASTPASSES," Lawson explained. He held his up to show her.

"They don't use paper FASTPASSES anymore."

Lawson rolled his eyes. "That's why they call them 'magical'."

Gren laughed. "You sound like Roy."

"Who is Roy?"

"He's a friend who works here," Gren told her. "He's the one who gave us the passes. They don't have an expiration date, so we should be able to use them today. Trust me, Winnie. It's the most incredible ride ever."

Winnie paused. "Will you hold my hand?"

"I won't let go."

"And promise me that nothing bad will happen?"

"I promise, Winnie."

"Okay," Winnie said at last. "I'll ride it."

Much to Gren's surprise, Roy was not working at the ride. She had been sure that they were about to see him. Instead, there was a woman named Cassidy who asked to see their tickets. Gren was pretty sure that Cassidy was the one who picked the third ticket up off of the ground a few minutes earlier. Cassidy looked at the FASTPASSES and then gave them back. She was very friendly but seemed to be a little bit on the spacy side. Cassidy was also there when it came time to board the ride. Gren and Winnie were seated in the last row, Lawson sat in the row in front of them. Even though there were plenty of people in the single rider line, no one was paired with Lawson.

"Have you put those tickets away?" Cassidy asked as she checked their harnesses.

Gren and Lawson both nodded. Winnie took Gren's hand, she was shaking. "Winnie, honey, there's nothing to worry about," Cassidy said. "Just put your head back and enjoy the ride."

"How do you know my name?" Winnie asked, but Cassidy was gone.

Lawson turned his head and flashed Gren one last smile. She put her head back and closed her eyes. As the countdown started, she wondered if her previous experience on the ride had somehow been a dream...a dream that could be wandered.

Introduction

Gren looked directly at Mollie. "Can we talk for a hundred or two? Just you and me?"

Mollie appeared slightly anxious. "Winnie too?"

Gren smiled at her sister. "Winnie too." Gren walked into the cramped bedroom, the two young students following her. She closed the door behind them. "Have a seat."

"I'm sorry if it happened again," Mollie said, avoiding Gren's gaze. "I don't mean for it to happen. Winnie told me that you'd be able to help me. She said that you're the best that there is, that you received the highest marks ever from the Learning Center, and that you're apprenticing with Haas. That's all my parents needed to know, he's legendary. Will you be able to help?"

"I'll do my best," Gren promised, placing a reassuring hand on Mollie's leg. "But first, tell me exactly what is happening. As you perceive it."

"My dreams sometimes come true," Mollie said slowly. "Sometimes it's just little things, but sometimes they're really important. "

Chapter One

A young girl sat by herself in the middle of the woods, crying. She buried her head in her lap and sobbed openly. "I—want—my—Mommy!" The child was having a difficult time catching her breath.

Gren tried hard to keep her voice calm and soothing. "Your Mommy is looking for you. You need to find her. Stand up and—"

"No!" the girl insisted. She kept her head down. "I don't want to stand up."

"Then look up." Gren's voice wavered slightly. "There's a bridge, right in front of you. Your Mommy is on the other side."

"No!" The child stopped crying but refused to look in the direction of the bridge. "I don't want to look for a bridge."

"Then listen..." Gren paused for a micro. "Can't you hear that? It's your Mommy, calling you. But you need to let her know where you are."

"No!" the girl screamed. "I don't hear her, she's not calling me. I want her to find me *right now*! I want to see her."

Gren tried not to panic. She had no idea what the child's mother looked like. In some instances that wouldn't matter but she knew that this time, it would. "Is that her? Over there, behind that tree?"

"No!" the girl replied. Her fear was gone, replaced by defiance. "That's my Aunt Bertha, and I don't even like her. *I want my Mommy*! I want her now!"

"If you just tell me what she looks like..." Everything immediately went dark. Gren knew that she had made a terrible mistake.

○ ○ ○●○ ○ ○

"No, no, no, no, no!" Haas shook his head as he stared hard at Gren. "This is exactly why I don't like to accept apprentices. But with you it was a personal request from Ladinda. She said you had so much promise. Tell me, Gren, what did you do wrong?"

"I...I..."

"Do you *always* have such a hard time finding the words?" Haas asked sarcastically. "Don't answer that. Answer this instead. How are you going to gain a client's, a *child's* trust if you have to ask questions? *You* were supposed to be guiding *her*, not the other way around."

Gren swallowed hard, determined not to cry. Crying only made Haas harder on her. "Excuse me, Sir, but in a clinical setting wouldn't I have already met the child's mother? I would know what she looks like, so it wouldn't be a problem."

"Not always," Haas replied, his tone remaining stern. "You might have met the father, or a grandparent, or the big brother. Alternatively, it could have been one of a dozen different people the girl was asking for. It just happened that this time she wanted her mother."

"So what should I have done?" Gren asked. "How would you have handled it?"

"The Wanderer is supposed to be guiding the child," Haas

said. "So I would have guided her."

"But she—"

"I also would never have referred to the child's mother as "Mommy". You're not her friend, you're her guide."

"But I—"

"Enough." Haas held up a hand. "You're going to need a lot more practice, Gren, before you're ready to even observe a real wandering session. Lawson, you'll be observing tomorrow. I will give you your instructions in the morning. Make sure you get plenty of rest. A *real* session can be intense, unlike what you're used to at the Learning Center." Haas stood and walked towards the door, mumbling to himself as he went. "I never wanted to accept apprentices, but no, Ladinda told me that this one was different. She said that she hadn't seen someone with so much potential in orbits. So I went out and bought a simulator…"

◦ ◦ ◦●◦ ◦ ◦

"I don't want to talk about it." Gren crossed her arms in front of her so that Lawson couldn't take her hand. "I want to talk about something else."

"Like what?" Lawson was having a hard time getting used to Gren's moods. He hated seeing her constantly upset.

"I don't know…the weather," Gren replied, anger in her voice. When they had been in school she had always been the best, the top of the class, and she wasn't used to struggling.

"It is a nice evening. Maybe we could grab a picnic for our evening meal, something simple, and find a nice spot to just sit. Not even talk, just enjoy each other's company. Like we used to. I'll even cook if you want."

"It's just not fair!" Gren burst out. "It's not even a real

dream, it a simulation. I could do a lot better wandering a real dream. But no, it's some stupid program. How am I supposed to get any practice from a stupid simulated program?"

Lawson put his hand on Gren's shoulder. "You'll get there. I think Haas is being so hard on you because he knows how great you're going to be. He's the best Dream Wanderer in the business, and my guess is that he feels threatened by your talent."

"Yeah, right. The Great Haas, Terra's best Dream Wanderer, scared of me." They stopped in front of a building. Gren lived by herself in a security building that was mostly single women living alone. Lawson lived on the same street, sharing a first-floor dwelling with Sham and Titus, his former school roommates. "Look, Lawson, is it okay if we don't have our meal together? I kind of want to be alone. Plus with Winnie and her partner coming in a few rotations, I need to move things around a bit. I still have to figure out where everyone is going to stay."

"You'll get plenty of practice when your sister is here," Lawson said. "Winnie is a good kid—it's going to be fun having her around. Plus since she's studying culinary arts, we might pick up a trade secret or two."

Gren almost smiled. "She's in her first orbit—I doubt that she knows many secrets. But it will be good having her around. Calli and Tayo too. It's really nice of them to volunteer to spend their break helping me out."

"The whole gang, together again." Things had become a bit strained between Gren and Lawson, and he wasn't sure how to fix it. Lawson shifted his weight from one foot to the other; he had gained a whole new appreciation for the Learning Center and its rules. Everything there had been spelled out; do this, don't do that, no physical contact allowed between students of the opposite gender. Haas had told them their first orbit that they weren't allowed to officially date while they were apprenticing, but other than that, they had a lot of freedom. "Do you need any help moving things around?" Lawson asked after a long, awkward silence.

"No, I can handle it." Gren looked at her best friend. "Stop worrying about me, Lawson. I'm okay. I just need to think."

"If you need me…"

"I'm fine." Gren touched Lawson's arm. It still felt strange to be able to do so. "I know where you are. But now, you'd better get going, before Sham eats all the food." She wasn't sure why she said that, she just really wanted Lawson to leave.

Lawson took the hint. "I'll see you in the morning." He reached over and squeezed Gren's hand before walking away.

"When *you* get to observe," Gren muttered as soon as she was sure that Lawson was out of earshot.

∘ ∘ ●◐◑ ∘ ∘

"It was so great!" Sham couldn't contain his excitement. He and Titus apprenticed for one of Haas' competitors. "This kid was about six orbits old, and Cassidy allowed me to wander his dream with no assistance, she just observed. A real dream too, not one induced by sleep tonic. He was having this nightmare about—"

"Sham," Titus interrupted, glancing at Lawson, "you know you're not allowed to talk about what happened in the dream. At least not to someone who wasn't there. The confidentiality cause, remember?"

"Oh, yeah, I forgot about that. But it was just *so great*! I felt like a real Dream Wanderer. I know that I really helped the kid.

How about you, Lawson? How was your rotation?"

"Whatever," Lawson replied. "Haas said that I can finally observe tomorrow."

"Observe?" Sham suppressed a laugh. "Titus and I have been observing for a whole lunar cycle!"

"Haas and the people in his practice have the reputation for being the best," Titus said, trying to avoid the argument that he knew was coming. "Lawson and Gren are the first apprentices that he's taken in almost two decades. It's not surprising if he's being cautious."

"Cautious?" Sham couldn't hold the laughter in any longer. "How much damage can a silent observer do? I don't care what his reputation is, if he's keeping Gren working in front of a simulator—he has no idea what he's doing."

Lawson, his fist clenched, took a step towards Sham. "You leave Gren out of this! She's doing the best that she can, she's trying her hardest!"

Sham stood and faced Lawson. "You're just upset because the two of you still can't be together. 'From one set of stupid rules to another'; you've said it yourself. You gave up your own dream to be near her and you still can only be friends. And you know what? It's about time that Gren had to *work* to get ahead, just like the rest of us. It's good that Haas won't let her just glide by on talent alone, like she's always done."

"Why you—"

Titus stepped between his two roommates just as Lawson took a swing. Lawson missed Sham and instead hit Titus squarely on the jaw. Titus fell to the floor.

"Look what you did!" Sham yelled. He rushed to his friend's side. "Titus, are you okay?"

Titus sat up and rubbed his jaw. "I am *really* getting sick of this conversation. Can we just finally agree that we're apprenticing under different approaches? No one is absolutely right and no one is wrong. If Haas wants to be more cautious, that's his prerogative. There's a reason that he's considered the best."

Lawson sat down on the floor next to Titus. "It's just so frustrating, you know? Gren is really discouraged. I've never seen her like this before. Haas is incredibly hard on her, worse than he is with me. She's becoming withdrawn, even from me, and I don't like what it's doing to her." He glanced at Sham. "You're right; she's used to being the best. She is so talented and has always been able to do whatever she set her mind to."

"Maybe that's why Haas is hard on her," Titus said. "Maybe he sees how great she's going to be."

Lawson nodded. "That's what I said to her."

Sham sat down next to them. "I'm sorry. I didn't mean to get you mad. It's just, I don't know, I was so excited about my rotation, and this whole thing with Gren always brings the mood down."

"'*Always* brings the mood down?'" Lawson repeated. "Do I talk about it that much?"

Sham and Titus both nodded.

"I didn't realize I was doing that," Lawson said. "I'll try to not bring it home with me. It's just so—"

"Frustrating," Titus and Sham replied together.

"Yeah." Lawson looked at Titus and grinned. "I'm sorry I hit you. I can't believe that I did that. But, you know, it was Sham's fault."

Titus rubbed his jaw again. "I know."

Chapter Two

Gren sat back and stared blankly ahead. She wasn't sure what she was supposed to be learning. She wasn't allowed to enter the dream, just watch Lawson as he observed. Haas was doing the actual wandering, speaking aloud as he did so. Gren found his approach annoying; she much preferred to wander silently. Then again, it had been so long since she had wandered an actual dream that she doubted she even remembered how to do it. A boy of about four orbits was lying on a bed, sound asleep. He was in a different room and could be seen on a monitor. The boy's mother sat next to him.

"Continue to walk forward," Haas instructed. There was a pause. "No, you won't fall. Hold onto the side rail." Haas paused again. "That's better. You won't lose your grip. Just keep going forward. When you reach the other side I want you to…"

Gren let her thoughts slip away. She glanced at Lawson. He sat with his eyes closed, observing again. He had observed three rotations in a row. *It's not fair!* Gren thought to herself. She was so sick of the simulator that she was starting to doubt her desire to become a licensed Dream Wanderer. It no longer seemed worth it.

"No!" Haas said. His voice was calm but filled with

authority. "You are not going to let go. Just continue forward and follow my instructions."

I can't wait until Winnie gets here, Gren thought. She's told me so much about her partner. It's going to be great to meet her. I wish I was looking forward to seeing Calli and Tayo, but they're going to be so full of questions. What am I supposed to tell them? That being an apprentice stinks, and that they should consider changing careers before they make the mistake of graduating? That Ladinda didn't teach us anything about how life really works? I shouldn't complain about them being here. They're doing me a favor by coming. They're giving up their break so that Winnie and her partner will have something to do while I'm at work. At least they won't have to sit here and watch me while I sit here and watch Lawson observe. Does Haas have any idea how boring this is?

"Gren!" Haas stood right in front of her. It was obvious that he had said her name several times. "You're supposed to be paying attention, not thinking about how bored you are."

"I..." Gren wasn't sure if Haas had wandered into her thoughts or not. It was possible to wander someone who was awake if they had allowed their mind to drift, she and Lawson had perfected it their last orbit at the Learning Center. "I'm sorry."

"You'd better be. You're going to have to try a lot hard if you ever think that you're going to be able to observe. Remember, Gren, your career and your future are in *my* hands. I'm going to set up the simulator for you. Lawson, you are to discuss what you observed with Gren."

"Yes, Sir," Lawson said. "See, Gren, the boy is scared of falling. He hurt himself badly in a terrible fall about half an orbit ago, and Haas is working to get him over that fear. He is slowly trying to…"

Gren's mind started to drift again, but instead of thinking about being bored, she concentrated on her anger.

• ◦ ●◗◐ ◦ ◦

Silently Gren and Lawson walked towards the station. Lawson tried to reach for Gren's hand but she pulled it away. "Calli and Tayo are going to meet us here?" Lawson asked, knowing the answer.

"Yeah," Gren replied. They entered the building.

"I'm glad Calli has a glidemobile." Lawson saw a couple of empty seats and headed in that direction. "It will be nice to not have to walk all the time."

"They're not coming here for you," Gren snapped. "They're coming to help me out with my sister and her partner, so they don't have to sit around and watch me do nothing all rotation, every rotation."

"Gren, I never said that they were coming for me." Lawson recognized Gren's mood and dreaded the outcome.

"You didn't have to. I know you, remember?"

Lawson took a deep breath before speaking again. "So the evening meal tonight at my place? All of us? Sham and Titus can't wait to see Calli and Tayo again."

"They're not coming here for Sham and Titus either. Honestly, I don't know what it is about you guys. You make everything about *you*. Well, the truth is that my little sister and her partner are coming here to see *me*, not you, the same with Calli and Tayo. *Maybe* we'll find a few micros to say hello sometime in the next few rotations, but why you expect us to have our lives revolve around you…"

"Okay, Gren. Enough." Lawson knew very well what it was like to be totally annoyed with a situation, he almost felt as if their roles from their last orbit at the Learning Center had reversed, but he had his limits. "You ask Calli and Tayo, I bet they *want* to see Titus and Sham. And as far as Winnie is concerned…"

Gren stood and faced her former partner. "You leave my little sister out of this!"

"I've known Winnie nearly her entire life! She may be your sister, but she's my friend. You know that I adore that kid. I've spent almost as much time with her as you have. You've said it yourself plenty of times; she enjoys having me around."

"Are you saying that I'm jealous?"

Lawson shook his head and tried to remain calm. "I didn't say that! I know you're upset about the way things are going with Haas, but Gren…"

"What does this have to do with Haas?" Gren turned her head away so that Lawson couldn't see her wipe away a tear. She faced him again. "We were talking about how you've managed to firmly plant yourself in my sister's life. *My* sister, not yours."

"Why don't you just mention your entire family?" Lawson no longer kept his voice down. "How I spent all my breaks with you when we were at the Learning Center? How your mom would always fuss over me, ask me what I wanted to eat, saying that she was going to 'fatten me up'? Or how your dad still calls me 'son'? Come on, Gren, I always saw the look on your face, I know it bothered you. Admit it."

"I never said that it bothered me! For your information, I always liked having you around. I think that's part of the reason we made it all the way through the program as partners, because we were so close."

Lawson didn't even try to hide his disappointment. "Were?"

"Things are so different now!" Gren glanced around and noticed several people staring. She lowered her voice. "We're adults; we need to start acting like it."

Lawson unintentionally rolled his eyes. "How, by fighting in the station?"

"We're not fighting!"

"Whatever you say, Gren." Lawson shook his head again. "As always."

"What's that supposed to mean?"

"Hi!" Calli's voice caused Gren to jump. "What's going on?"

"Yeah," Tayo said. "We could hear the two of you outside. You sounded just like *we* used to."

Gren glanced longingly for a micro at the blue uniforms that the two girls were wearing. How she missed the Learning Center! "Come here," she said, throwing her arms around her former roommates. The three girls embraced for several micros.

"My turn," Lawson said at last. Calli looked at him as if he had lost his mind. "It's okay, I'm a *former* student. The 'no contact' rule no longer applies. See?" He touched Gren gently on the shoulder. "We didn't explode, and Terra didn't stop spinning."

"Okay," Tayo said. She and Calli cautiously approached Lawson and barely touched his arm.

"That was worth it," he said sarcastically.

* ∘ ⦿●◉●∘ ∘

The friends talked for several hundreds while waiting for Gren's sister to arrive. Calli and Tayo quickly realized that there were subjects that they needed to avoid. They noticed that Gren had changed. She seemed so down. Lawson, on the other hand, had developed a newfound sense of confidence.

"When are we going to see Sham and Titus?" Calli asked.

"Tonight, for the evening meal," Gren replied. She shot Lawson a nasty look. "We're going to go over to the guys' place. They have more room. Where I'm living, well, it's fine for one person, but with five of us staying there things are going to be kind of tight."

"Hey, is that Winnie?" Lawson pointed at two young girls, each struggling with a traveling case.

Gren stood immediately and ran over to her sister. She picked her up and swung her around. "Winnie, it's so great that you're here! We're going to have such a good time!" With long red hair, it was obvious that Winnie and Gren were related.

Winnie laughed as her sister put her back down. She then gave Lawson a heart-felt hug. "Everybody, this is Mollie, my partner. Mollie, this is Gren and her friends Lawson, Calli, and Tayo."

"It's very nice to meet all of you," Mollie said. She was quite a bit smaller than Winnie, with shoulder length black hair and dark, sad eyes.

Gren was immediately impressed with how polite Mollie was. "Look at the two of you. You look great. I can't believe that my little sister is a White."

Winnie twirled around to show off her uniform. The styles were different from the Dream Wandering Learning Center, but most of the educational institutions on Terra had adopted the same color system to identify the students' orbit.

"Here, Mollie, let me take that for you." Lawson took

Mollie's traveling case as Gren took her sister's things. "Did you have a good trip?"

"Yes, thank you," Mollie replied.

"We're going to head to my place, get everyone settled in," Gren said. "Then in a couple of units we'll go over to Lawson's. We're going to have the evening meal over there."

"Yeah, kid, since you're studying culinary arts I thought I'd let you do all of the cooking while you're here."

Winnie laughed. "Lawson, you're so funny. Most of our classes have nothing to do with cooking." She smiled at Mollie.

"'You're here to receive a full, well-rounded education, not just learn how to cook,'" they said together, obviously imitating someone.

"But," Winnie continued by herself, "if you need us to measure something, we would be more than happy to help out. We're at the top of our class in measuring."

Lawson shot a quick look at Gren. He knew that she was thinking about how she had always been at the top of their class in everything.

Chapter Three

After an enjoyable evening Gren and all the girls headed back to her place. Her dwelling was small, but she had managed to find enough room for everyone. She had borrowed some cots from her neighbors; two of them were set up in her bedroom while the other two were in the main living area.

"Okay, Gren, tell us what's going on." Calli had waited until the giggling in the other room had died down before approaching the subject.

"I don't know what you mean," Gren lied.

"Gren, it's us," Tayo said. "We've been through so much together. We know you better than just about anyone."

"Holy splarsh, you sound like Lawson."

Tayo gasped at Gren's use of the impolite expression.

"See," Calli said, "you even saying that shows that something is wrong. And you were fighting with Lawson. In public! I never expected to walk in on a scene like that."

"Lawson and I used to fight all the time," Gren said. "Back at the Learning Center."

"Yeah, but this was different." Calli paused. "That was usually because Lawson hated the 'no contact' rule so much. This time—I don't know, Gren, but it sounded like you were the one who started it."

"He...he..." Gren sighed. "I'm snapping at him all the time lately. It's not even his fault, at least not most of the time. It's just not fair! Sham and Titus are already wandering, Lawson is observing, and me? I'm stuck with the stupid simulator! Then Haas will remind me that he didn't even own the stinking thing before Ladinda came to him and told him how talented I'm *supposed* to be. I can't even remember the last time I wandered, it's been so long."

"So why are you taking it out on Lawson?" Tayo asked.

"Because he...he...I'm the one who is supposed to be observing by now, not him! The whole time we were at the Learning Center he had to struggle to keep up with me, not the other was around!"

"So you're mad at Lawson because he's doing well? Gren, that's not fair to him and you know it." Calli hoped she wouldn't regret her words.

"I'm not mad at Lawson," Gren said slowly. "Not really. He's just...there. You're right—I'm not being fair to him. I guess he and I should talk or something."

"That's probably not a bad idea," Tayo said. "You and Lawson have always been so close; I know he'd want to help you through this."

"So how are you and Lawson doing?" Calli asked. "You know, otherwise?"

Gren shook her head. "If you're referring to the fact that you both always thought that Lawson and I would end up joined, Haas has strictly forbidden us to date. Which is just as well, we need to concentrate on our apprenticeships. There's a huge gray area here, things aren't black and white like they've been for most of the time that we've known each other. Lawson seems to like the gray area and you know him, he'll test the boundaries. Good thing I'm more sensible than he is. So...how are things at the Learning Center? Has Ladinda come up with any strange new rules that she claims are for everyone's good but doesn't bother to explain?"

Noticing Gren's obvious attempt to change the subject, Tayo and Calli grinned at each other.

⚬ ⚬ ◯ ⬤ ◯ ⚬ ⚬

In the other room, the two younger girls were speaking in hushed tones. "Do you really think she'll be able to help?" Mollie asked. "That she'll want to help?"

"I know she will." Winnie replied. "Did you give her the permission form from your parents?"

"Oh, no, it's still in my bag," Mollie said. "I'll give it to her tomorrow."

"Are you sure you don't want to tell her what's going on?"

Mollie shook her head. "No. I think it's better if she finds out on her own."

"Okay, I won't say anything to her." Winnie put her head on her pillow. "Try to get some sleep. It's been a long rotation."

"If it happens, you'll get her?" Mollie asked.

"Of course."

"Promise?"

"I promise."

⚬ ⚬ ◯ ⬤ ◯ ⚬ ⚬

"We're hoping to apprentice together," Tayo explained quietly. "We've sent out a few inquiries and had a couple of replies, but so far we're pretty much keeping our options open."

"We don't really want to go too far away," Calli added. "We'd like to try to be kind of close to our families..."

"Without losing our independence," Tayo said. She glanced around the dimly lit room. "Being our on own is going to be great."

Gren laughed. "Listen to you two. Who would have thought an orbit ago that you'd be making plans to stick together past graduation?"

The two Blues exchanged a quick smile. "It's all thanks to Ladinda," Calli said. "Her leadership at the Learning Center has made all the difference."

There was a gentle knock on the door. "Gren, are you awake?" Winnie asked quietly.

"Come in, we're still up," Gren said to her sister. Winnie entered the crowded room and Gren motioned for her sister to sit on the end of the bed. "What's up?"

"It's Mollie," Winnie replied. "It's happening again."

"What's happening?"

"Maybe you should just come with me." Winnie grabbed Gren's hand and pulled. Gren followed her sister into the other room. Mollie was sitting up on the cot. Her eyes were open and fixed straight ahead.

"Mollie?" Gren said quietly. "Is everything okay?"

"She's dreaming," Winnie explained. "I know it doesn't look like it, but she is. She wants you to wander when she's like this."

"Winnie, honey, I can't," Gren said. "I don't have permission—it's against the law."

"Hold on." Winnie pulled Mollie's bag out from under the cot and opened it. She rummaged through her partner's things. "Here," she said at last, handing Gren a piece of paper. "Permission from Mollie and her parents. They want you to try to wander. Mollie just mentioned it to me before she fell asleep.

Please, Gren."

Gren read the paper. It stated that only Gren had permission to wander, but she was allowed to discuss the dreams. Gren sat down on the end of her sister's cot. "Okay. Winnie, you can sit next to me." She glanced up at Calli and Tayo, who were standing in the doorway. "Why don't you guys go ahead and go to bed? I'll be in as soon as I'm done." Gren didn't want to admit it, but she didn't want her former roommates to watch. She didn't want them to see how badly her skills had deteriorated.

∘ ∘ ● ● ∘ ∘ ∘

"Is everything okay?" Calli asked. She was lying on her cot, the covers pulled up tightly around her. "I've never seen anyone dream like that before."

"Me either," Tayo added. She, too, was lying down. Gren was standing in the doorway, a strange look on her face.

Gren was confused. She knew that she had entered Mollie's dream, that the scene in front of her wasn't really happening. She had seen herself in dreams before, but this was different. She continued to search the dream; something was missing. After a micro she realized that Mollie wasn't there. "Mollie?" she called out. She knew that she shouldn't, one of the rules of wandering was that you shouldn't refer to the dreamer by name. Gren had never understood that rule, she had used her friends' names in their dreams several times without any problems. "Mollie, are you here?"

Everything went black.

∘ ∘ ● ● ∘ ∘ ∘

"How often does it happen?" Gren asked her sister. After calling out Mollie's name, the girl had apparently stopped dreaming.

"It varies," Winnie replied. "It happens more often when she's nervous or excited about something. I think that spending the break here probably had something to do with it, it's been all that she's been able to talk about for rotations."

"Well," Gren said, standing up, "you try to get some sleep. If it happens again, let me know." She kissed her sister on the top of her head before heading back into the bedroom.

• ◦ ◍ ◑ ◌ ◦ ◦

"Is everything okay?" Calli asked. She was lying on her cot, the covers pulled up tightly around her. "I've never seen anyone dream like that before."

"Me either," Tayo added. She, too, was lying down.

Gren stood in the doorway and stared straight ahead. "What did you two just say?"

"We asked if Mollie was okay," Calli repeated.

"But now I'm going to ask about you," Tayo said. "Gren, what's wrong? You look like you've seen a ghost."

Gren sat down slowly on her bed. "Not a ghost. But what you two just said? It was word for word from Mollie's dream. Exactly the same. It was almost as if she was dreaming the future."

Chapter Four

Gren had wanted to ask Mollie about the dream before leaving for her apprenticeship work, but everyone was still asleep. Instead, she stood outside of her building, waiting for Lawson to show up. She finally saw him in the distance, walking towards her. She ran to meet him. "Lawson, what took you so long?" she asked. "You're late."

Lawson squinted at his friend. "What are you talking about? I'm still a couple of hundreds early. Besides, you're the one who has consistently been late. Almost every rotation this lunar cycle!"

"Whatever." Gren pulled Lawson's arm. "Come on, I need to talk to you. The strangest thing happened last night."

On the short walk to work Gren told Lawson about Mollie's dream. "I would tell Haas about it," Lawson said outside the door. "He might know what's going on."

"No," Gren said. "Lawson, promise me you won't say anything to him unless I do."

"It's your call. However you want to handle it is totally up to you." Lawson smiled. It was nice to see Gren excited about something.

　　　　　　　　∘ ◦ ● ◉ ● ◦ ∘

Gren paid closer attention as she watched Haas wander a young girl's dream. Although she wasn't allowed to observe the dream, she thought that maybe she could pick something up. Even though she didn't personally like the man, she knew that there had to be a reason for his reputation. There was nothing different, nothing she hadn't seen countless times before.

"Come," Haas said when the session was over. "I'm going to set up the simulator."

Gren and Lawson followed. There was a question on her mind, something about Mollie's dream that made no sense to her. She decided to just come out and ask. "Sir, why can't we call people by name if we're wandering?"

Haas stared hard at Gren, making her feel very small. "You wouldn't do that, would you? I had thought that with your supposed skills you would know…it's one thing if it's someone you know very well. Wandering the dream of a close friend is different than a real session. That's one of the problems with the Learning Center—it's mostly your partner's dreams that you practice wandering. In a *real* session, it's different. The sleeper's mind doesn't process things as they would if they were awake. If you're wandering their dream, they perceive you as their conscious. Would your conscious call you by name? Even if yours would, there are enough people, *especially* children, that wouldn't understand. It could end the dream immediately, possibly even break further trust. *Never* refer to someone by name in a dream, especially a child."

Gren nodded, finally understanding. She had been told for orbits that you don't call someone by name when wandering, but no one had ever before explained why. She also understood why Mollie's dream had ended so abruptly. "Another question, Sir, if you don't mind. Does the dreamer have to be in a dream?"

"No," Haas replied. "The older the child, the more likely that they will be in the dream, but it doesn't always happen. Why all the questions, Gren? Has something happened?"

Gren thought quickly. She still didn't want to tell Haas about Mollie's dream. "My sister and her friend are here, and I was planning on practicing, as you had suggested. I've never met her partner before, but her parents have given permission for me to wander, and we were talking last night. She said that she doesn't always appear in her own dreams."

"It makes things more difficult for the Wanderer," Haas explained, some of the harshness gone from his voice. "If you wander and she's not in the dream, remark on what you *do* see. Just let her know that you're there, as a guiding voice, then see what plays out. Is the child plagued by nightmares?"

"Not that I know of," Gren replied.

"If she is," Haas said, "bring her in. I would be willing to give her a free session. I might even let you observe."

"I'm sorry, Sir," Gren said slowly, "but her parents only gave permission to me."

"Fine." The gruffness was back in Haas' voice. "I don't have the extra time anyway, since I suddenly have found myself babysitting a couple of apprentices. The simulator is set. Are you ready?"

"Yes, Sir," Gren said. She decided to keep her final question to herself and not ask him if dreams ever came true.

∘ ∘ ◉◉ ∘ ∘

After a long rotation at work that seemed like it would never end, Lawson finally walked Gren home. He was happy that she let him hold her hand. "You want to meet again tonight?" he asked. "The evening meal? I know that Winnie enjoyed it last night. That sister of yours, she's quite a…"

"Yeah, sure, whatever," Gren replied. "Um, Lawson, do you want to meet again tonight? We could have the evening meal together again, all of us."

Lawson grinned. "Why didn't I think of that?"

"We'll meet you over at your place in a couple of units," Gren said. "Okay?"

"Sounds good to me," Lawson replied. "I'll let Sham and Titus know. They won't have any problem with it."

"See you then." Gren gave Lawson a quick kiss on the cheek before running up the steps of her building.

∘ ∘ ● ● ∘ ∘ ∘

Gren was disappointed that no one was at her place. Calli had left a note, explaining that they had gone out to do some sightseeing and would be back well before the evening meal. Still wanting answers, Gren took a box out of the closet. It contained some of her old books from the Learning Center and other books about wandering that she had always intended to read, but had never found the time. She glanced through several of them before finding one that looked promising.

"Let me see," Gren said aloud. She sat down in a chair and pulled up her legs. "'Dream Wanderers are specially trained individuals who will help people through their dreams. It's used as a form of therapy'…I know all this…'wandering can help people of all ages'…blah blah blah…'there have been occasional reports of dreams coming true. This is not possible. Dreams are the subconscious mind's way of working something out. If something happens in a dream that later happens in real life it would have happened anyway. The phenomenon is referred to as Self Fulfilling Prophecy. See page 713 for more information.'" Gren closed the book without turning to page 713. "How can it be self-fulfilling if the person who had the dream isn't in it?" She put her head back, closed her eyes, and pondered the question.

○ ◦ ● ● ◐ ◦ ○

"Dreams coming true?" Haas stood over Gren, staring down at her. She was sitting on the floor. Lawson was behind him. "Where have you heard of such nonsense?"

"I...I..."

"Enough!" Haas pointed his finger at Gren. "I don't know where you come up with these ideas. Ladinda told me that you had so much promise, but no. You think that you're better than everyone else. You think that you're a better Dream Wanderer than I am!" Haas laughed. "You're no longer my apprentice. Lawson can stay, he's doing a superb job *and* he hasn't come up with crazy ideas about dreams coming true. But you? I want you out of here within the unit or I'm going to call security."

"Where am I supposed to go?" Gren asked.

"Why should I care?" Haas laughed again. "Go beg on the street. Or better yet, scare little children. Tell them that their dreams might come true. That will bring more business *my* way. I'll need more help. Maybe I didn't waste all that money on the simulator after all. Lawson, do you know of anyone else who would want to apprentice?"

"Sure," Lawson said. Calli and Tayo appeared in the room.

"Good." Haas turned his attention to the two girls. "Follow me, I'll show you around." They left the room.

Lawson squatted down next to Gren. "Sorry, Gren. It's nothing personal. I just can't have you dragging me down with your crazy ideas. Dreams coming true..."

"Gren, wake up!" Winnie was shaking her sister's shoulder. "We've had a really great rotation. Calli and Tayo took us to four different restaurants. Four! When we told them that Mollie and I are studying at the Culinary Institute all four gave us a tour of the kitchen. Mollie and I are going to have so much to brag about when we get back."

"And I brought food," Calli said, holding up a bag. "The last place gave it to us, for free! Are we eating with the guys again this evening? There's plenty for everyone."

"Huh?" Gren rubbed the sleep out of her eyes. She placed the book on the floor. "Oh, the guys. Yeah. I told Lawson we'd meet him over there sometime around now."

"What are we waiting for?" Calli asked. "Let's go."

"Wait a micro." Gren looked directly at Mollie. "Can we talk for a hundred or two? Just you and me?"

Mollie appeared slightly anxious. "Winnie too?"

Gren smiled at her sister. "Winnie too." Gren walked into the cramped bedroom, the two young students following her. She closed the door behind them. "Have a seat."

"I'm sorry if it happened again," Mollie said, avoiding Gren's gaze. "I don't mean for it to happen. Winnie told me that you'd be able to help me. She said that you're the best that there is, that you received the highest marks ever from the Learning Center, and that you're apprenticing with Haas. That's all my parents needed to know, he's legendary. Will you be able to help?"

"I'll do my best," Gren promised, placing a reassuring hand on Mollie's leg. "But first, tell me exactly what is happening. As you perceive it."

"My dreams sometimes come true," Mollie said slowly. "Sometimes it's just little things, but sometimes they're really important. Winnie tells me that I sit up in bed when I have these dreams."

"It happens every time," Winnie added. "That's how I knew to get you last night. I knew it was happening."

"Do you remember the dream after it's over?" Gren asked.

"Maybe for a few micros but they fade quickly," Mollie replied. "Winnie and I have kind of come up with a system. When it happens, I tell Winnie the dream and she writes it down immediately. We keep track of them in a journal."

Gren grew excited. "Did you bring the journal with you?"

"Yeah," Winnie said, "it's in the other room. Hold on a micro."

It seemed to take forever for Winnie to get the dream journal and return with it. Gren flipped through it. She ignored the fact that her sister's penmanship wasn't the greatest and all the spelling errors. After all, her sister was still a new student. Language Arts was one of her many classes.

"All of these dreams have come true?" Gren asked Mollie.

Mollie nodded. "What does it mean?"

"I'm not really sure." Gren closed the journal and laid it in her lap. "If you're not uncomfortable talking about it, I'd like to discuss it with my friends tonight. The permission form from your parents said that I'm the only one allowed to wander, but that it is okay to talk about it."

"I trust Winnie," Mollie said slowly. "She said that I can also trust you and your friends, and so I do. But this isn't something that I want everyone knowing about. My mom is scared that if people find out, I'll be exploited."

Gren immediately thought that "exploited" was a pretty big word for such a small girl to be worried about. "You can trust me, Mollie, and my friends. We'll do our best to figure out what is going on."

"Can you make it stop?" Mollie asked. "That's what I want, for it to just go away. I don't want to be able to dream the future. I want to be a normal kid. Please, Gren, make it stop."

Gren patted Mollie on the leg. "I'll do my best.

Gren brought the journal with her when they went to Lawson's for the evening meal. After they had eaten, everyone sat around as Gren read from it. Although Lawson's place was bigger than Gren's, with eight people inside it was still somewhat cramped.

"Announcement at end of rotation that two Reds have been expelled from the program for fighting. Threw boiling water at each other." Gren flipped the page. "Thirty questions on the Math test, half of them have to do with measurements."

"Hey, that could come in handy!" Sham teased. He was sitting next to Calli. "Knowing the test ahead of time." He took his finger and touched Calli on the arm. "Poke."

Calli ignored him.

"We would never cheat," Winnie said.

"I know that, Winnie," Sham replied, slightly ashamed that he had said it. "I was just kidding." He touched Calli again. "Poke."

Calli ignored him.

"That's why I want it gone," Mollie added. "If others find out, kids will want us to help them cheat. Or the teachers will think that Winnie and I are cheating already.

Or..." Mollie's words dropped.

Gren flipped another page. "Glidemobile accident. Two people killed." She looked up at Mollie. "You saw it happen? That must have been horrible."

Mollie nodded. "At first we thought that it was just a regular nightmare. Then we heard about it a couple of rotations later. That dream I remembered, it didn't fade like most of the others do."

"Did you know the people involved?" Gren asked.

"No," Mollie replied. "Sometimes there's a connection—someone I've met or a friend of a friend, but there have been several dreams that Winnie and I haven't been able to connect to anyone that we know."

"Are you going to ask Haas about this?" Titus asked Gren.

"No," Gren said quickly. "He...he's busy. Besides, he's very old school when it comes to wandering. I don't think he'd believe it."

"Do you want us to talk to Cassidy?" Sham asked. He touched Calli again. "Poke."

Calli ignored him.

"Who's Cassidy?" Mollie asked.

"She's the Dream Wanderer that Titus and I are working for," Sham explained. "She's very broad minded when it comes to new ideas and theories. She might know what to do."

"I don't want to meet anyone else," Mollie said quickly. "And my parents only want Gren to wander."

"Relax," Sham said, almost sounding like he was wandering. "I won't mention anyone by name, not even Gren." He touched Calli again. "Poke."

Calli ignored him.

Mollie slowly nodded. "Okay. If you think she could help."

"It's worth a shot." Sham touched Calli again. "Poke."

"Would you stop!" Calli screamed at last.

Sham just laughed.

"Why does he keep doing that?" Winnie whispered to Gren.

Gren smiled. "Because the Learning Center has a rule. You're not allowed to touch a student of the opposite gender. Sham is no longer a student, so for the first time since he's known Calli, that rule doesn't apply."

"Oh," Winnie replied. "Boys. One of these rotations, will you explain them to me?"

"Little sister, you ask the impossible."

Chapter Five

Sham and Titus sat in Cassidy's office with the door closed. Titus was slightly worried that Cassidy would think that they were crazy, but Sham was fairly certain that she would understand. Cassidy's desk was a mess; covered with stacks of papers. The lights were low even though there was no window. Incense filled the air.

"So," Cassidy started, her voice low, "what did you two want to see me about? You're both doing remarkably well, if that's the problem. You've almost caught up to Grey, and he's been an apprentice a full orbit longer than you have. Of course, he tends to ignore what he's doing, always looking for the quick and easy way out of things. Can't have quick and easy when you're wandering!"

"It's not about our progress," Titus said slowly. "It's about a friend of a friend of a friend…well…sort of. We, um…"

"Is it possible for someone to have dreams that come true?" Sham blurted out. "Consistently?"

Cassidy looked at Sham over a pile of papers. "Do you know someone that this is happening to?"

"Well, sort of," Sham repeated. "She's a friend of a friend of a friend. Her parents know that we're apprenticing, and thought that maybe we could mention it."

"It's called Premonition Dreaming. This is remarkable!"

Cassidy exclaimed. "How old is she? How intense are the dreams? How long has this been happening?"

"I don't really know how long," Sham said. "She's still a kid, in her first orbit at her school."

Titus was relieved when he realized that Cassidy didn't think that they had lost their minds. "I'm not sure about the intensity," he added. "I think it varies. Her dreams have been as simple as a conversation, to as horrifying as the deaths of a couple of people in a glidemobile accident. People that she didn't even know."

"The ability to predict death." Cassidy stared straight ahead, lost in thought. "Amazing."

"Is it possible to, I don't know, get rid of these dreams?" Sham asked.

Cassidy looked surprised. "Why would she want to?"

"She wants to have a normal life," Sham explained. "Live the way a kid is supposed to live."

"Plus her parents are worried that she might be exploited," Titus added.

Cassidy nodded her head in agreement. "I hadn't thought of that. With the right combination of sleep tonics it might be possible to make the dreams happen more frequently. It would have to be a mixture of several different types of tonics, there's no exact science for this type of thing, especially since most professionals won't admit that the phenomenon even exists." She paused. "But to answer your question, yes, it is possible for these types of dreams to stop. It's a rare gift that the friend of your friend of your friend has been given, but it can be suppressed." She shuffled through some of the papers on her desk. "I'm sure that I have some information on this concept somewhere. Let me see what I can find, and I'll get back to you."

· · ● ● ● · ·

After leaving Cassidy's office Sham and Titus wanted to find a quiet place to talk. "That was very reassuring," Sham whispered as they walked. "Looks like she'll be able to help."

"I'm just glad she didn't throw us out," Titus said back. "I thought for sure that she would think that we're crazy *and* that we'd lose our apprenticeship."

"That wouldn't have happened." They rounded a corner. "Cassidy is very..." Sham stopped abruptly, having almost walked into Grey.

"Sham, Titus," Grey said while looking them over. "Together as always. I don't think I've ever seen one of you without the other."

"Cassidy decided that since we were partners at the Learning Center we should work together here," Sham said. Neither he nor Titus had ever liked Grey. He had been an orbit ahead of them at the Learning Center. He had always been a bit of a loner, even towards his school partner. "Not that it's any of your business."

Grey brushed his hair out of his eyes. "You were in talking with Cassidy long enough."

"Again, Grey, none of your business," Sham said.

"We had a question," Titus added, trying to defuse a bad situation before it started. "About practical practice. That's all."

Grey continued to stare at Sham. "As long you weren't trying to take over my wandering time. I've been watching you two. Ever since you got here, all you've done is try to take over. You know what? I'm sick of it! I was an apprentice here first, and I'm working hard, doing everything I can to get my license."

"That's not what Cassidy told us," Sham said.

"So you *were* talking to her about me! I should…" Grey rolled his hand up into a fist and took a swing at Sham. Titus, realizing what was going to happen, pushed his friend out of the way and ended up taking the full force of the punch. He fell to the floor. "I am so sick of that happening!" he screamed.

Sham helped Titus up while Grey stood there and laughed. Cassidy showed up behind them. She had a pile of books in her arms that she immediately gave to Sham. "What's going on here?" she asked.

"Nothing," the three young men replied.

Cassidy put her hands on her hips. "Grey, you have a wandering session in five hundreds. I'd suggest that you not be late this time."

Grey stood there, not moving.

"Sham, Titus, I found some information about that question you had. Grey, go!"

As Grey looked back, Sham mouthed the words, "I told you so," and Titus rubbed his jaw.

○ ○ ●◐ ○ ○

That evening everyone met again at Lawson's place. Winnie and Mollie played quietly in a corner while everyone else poured over the books.

"It says here that the future is shady," Titus said. "Premonition Dreaming isn't showing the future, the dreams show what will happen if events aren't changed."

"I don't know, that sounds like a cop-out," Sham said. "Like they're making excuses, in case the dream doesn't come true."

"You know, there's not one book here that Haas would say was written by a reputable Dream Wanderer," Lawson pointed out. Everyone ignored him.

"This one talks about a girl named Purcella that reported the same type of phenomenon about thirty orbits ago," Gren informed her friends. "One night when she was about five it started. Mollie, how long has this been going on?"

"It was right after I found out that I had been accepted at the Culinary Institute," Mollie replied. She and Winnie returned to what they were doing.

Gren smiled, it was nice to see them acting like kids.

"'Premonition Dreaming, while rare, can be brought on by stress,'" Calli read. She was purposely sitting far away from Sham so that he wouldn't be able to poke her. "Mollie, were you nervous about starting school?"

Winnie answered for her. "Who wouldn't be nervous about leaving home and starting school for a career that's been chosen for you based on a placement test that you took as a young child?"

"Good point."

Gren looked back at the book in front of her. "Purcella's family had just lost their home in a fire. The next night was when she had her first premonition dream."

"Losing your home, that's stress," Lawson commented.

Gren continued to read. "'It continued until…'" she lowered her voice to barely above a whisper, "'Purcella's suicide eight orbits later.'" She glanced up to make sure that her sister and Mollie hadn't heard. "It says here that the pressure was too much for her. Everyone was always expecting her to tell them what was going to happen." Gren turned the page and gasped.

"What is it?" Lawson asked.

Gren held up the book, careful to make sure that the girls in the corner couldn't see. There was a picture of Purcella. She looked exactly like Winnie.

Chapter Six

Haas was combing his hair. Gren felt a little bit strange watching, it was almost as if she was invading his personal space. "That's Haas," she said quietly. "He's one of the top Dream Wanderers in the business." Haas put away the comb and left his necessary room. Gren suppressed a sigh of relief; she had been very uncomfortable seeing a room that's supposed to be private. Haas entered another room, most likely the dwelling's main living area. It was huge. There were several expensive-looking paintings on the walls, the furniture was luxurious, and there were knickknacks everywhere. It was obvious that Haas was doing well for himself.

"Haas, honey," a female voice called, "could you come here for a micro?"

"I have to leave for work," Haas called back. "There's an important new client starting, and I need to work on my plan."

Gren knew that was true; the son of an important government official was supposed to have his first session in the morning.

"Plus I have to set things up for those two apprentices that Ladinda saddled me with. I don't know why I ever allowed her to talk me into…"

"Please, Haas," the woman called. "It will only take a micro."

"Fine." Haas ran up the stairs. At the top was an attractive woman, several orbits younger than Haas. Gren knew that Haas was joined, but had never even seen a picture of his wife. "What do you need?"

The woman pointed at a painting that was at the top of the stairs. "It's crooked."

"You're going to make me late for the most important rotation of my career because a painting is crooked?"

The woman pulled forward a clump of her blond hair and twirled it around her finger. She looked at Haas with her big blue eyes. "Please, Haas? You know that it will drive me crazy—it's just one of those things with me. I'd do it myself, but I can't reach." She moved closer to him and spoke in his ear, her voice just above a whisper. "I'm so lucky to have a tall, handsome husband like you."

Gren felt increasingly uncomfortable watching and considered calling Mollie by name. Instead, she remained silent.

Haas grinned at his wife. "Don't think that I don't realize it when you're playing me." He grabbed a nearby chair and moved it as close as he could to the painting. He climbed up onto the chair and made an adjustment. "Is that better?"

"Now it's higher on the right," his wife said. "Just a little bit." Haas moved the painting again. "Perfect. Thank you, honey."

Haas lowered himself slightly to get off the chair. As he did so, he lost his balance and tumbled down the stairs. "Holy splarsh!" he screamed. Everything went black.

· · ● ○ · ·

Gren told Lawson about the dream as they walked to work. "The last thing that I saw, Haas was rolling down the stairs.

That was when Mollie stopped dreaming."

"Has Mollie given you any type of time table?" Lawson asked.

"What do you mean?"

"Well, when she dreams something that we think is a premonition dream, does it happen right away? Or does it happen rotations later?"

Gren thought for a micro. "Lawson, I'm so stupid. I can't believe I hadn't thought to ask her that!"

Lawson chuckled. "Gren, the *last* thing that you are is stupid. There's just been so much going on, so much new information. You can't think of everything all at once."

"What do you think we should do?" Gren asked.

"About what?"

"One of the books last night said that the future is shady," Gren reminded him. "Should we warn Haas?"

"What, tell him not to stand on a chair if his wife says a picture is crooked? Yeah, Gren, you be the one to tell him."

Gren thought for a micro. "It's probably already happened. He said he didn't want to be late because of an important new client."

Lawson grinned. "Haas…late? Besides, he says every new client is important. It might not have been the government kid that he was talking about."

"That's true. And who knows. Maybe it wasn't a premonition dream. Mollie must have normal dreams too. Everyone does." They had arrived at their building so they opened the door and went in. They walked past the receptionist.

"Lawson, Gren," the woman called after them. "The office is closed for the next several rotations. You can go home. I'm leaving myself, as soon as I cancel all of Haas' appointments."

"Why, what's going on?" Lawson asked.

"Haas is in the Medical Center. He fell down a flight of stairs at his house and broke his leg in three places. He hurt his wrist as well."

"Is he okay?" Lawson asked. "Otherwise?"

"Yeah, there are no internal injuries or anything," the receptionist said. "But they're still going to keep him at the Medical Center for a couple of rotations, and then they're ordering him to take some time off. You know Haas, he's furious. Scared he's going to lose all his clients."

"Haas is the best in the business," Lawson said. "His clients all know that."

"True. Listen, I'll let you two know when to come back. Until then, enjoy your time off…with pay."

"Thanks." Lawson took a step towards the door.

Gren didn't move. "Do you know how he fell?"

"His wife said he fell off a chair at the top of the stairs. What he was doing, standing on a chair before work, I'll never understand."

Gren looked off into the distance. "He was straightening a painting."

The receptionist stared at Gren. "How would you know that?"

Gren thought quickly. She didn't want the woman to know that she had seen it happen through Mollie's dream. "It just makes sense. Haas makes a very good living; he probably has a lot of artwork and curios around his dwelling. A lot of rich people like to put expensive paintings at the top of the stairs, to show how well off they are." She glanced at Lawson. "Don't they?"

"Yeah," Lawson agreed quickly, trying to help Gren out of the jam. "At least I would think so. I wouldn't know from personal experience. Gren, come on, let's get going. We have an unexpected vacation, and that means you can spend more time with your sister." He grabbed Gren by the arm and pulled her towards the door.

• • •●• • •

Lawson knew exactly where Gren wanted to go, although he had been hoping she wouldn't suggest it. Gren held a small bouquet of flowers in her hand. She talked with a worker as Lawson stood off to the side. He hated medical centers ever since his parents had died when he was a young child.

"His room is this way," Gren said. She started walking down a hall, expecting Lawson to follow.

Lawson almost had to run to catch up. "Gren, do you really think that this is such a good idea? The poor man is in pain, and he's most likely more than a little bit embarrassed."

"Haas, embarrassed? He's probably going to find a way to blame this on me. Of course, it *is* my fault. I knew it was going to happen and I didn't do anything to stop it."

"What were you supposed to do, borrow Calli's glidemobile and run over to his place in the middle of the night? And he never would have believed you. Come on, Gren, think about it. There's nothing that you could have done."

Gren stopped in front of a door and lowered her voice. "This is it." She knocked.

A gruff voice answered. "Come in."

They entered the room and Gren put the flowers on a nearby table. "Haas, Sir…um…we just wanted to see how you are."

Haas looked terrible. One leg was elevated over the bed. His wrist was bandaged. There were several small scrapes and cuts everywhere, and both his eyes were black. "How do you think that I am?"

At least his voice wasn't damaged Lawson thought to himself. "We also wanted to wish you a speedy recovery."

"Speedy, or long?" Haas bellowed. "Don't think that I don't know that all my employees are happy about having an unexpected vacation."

"Haas, no," Gren said. "That's not it at all."

Haas stared at Gren. "I want you to put this time to good use. Wander your sister's dreams as much as possible. Her friend's too, the one who isn't in her own dreams. Practice, practice, practice. Then maybe, just maybe, when we get back, you'll be *close* to being able to observe. Maybe."

"Thank you, Sir, I will," Gren said. She and Lawson glanced at each other; they knew it was time to leave. "We hope you feel better, Sir."

"And we wish you a speedy recovery," Lawson repeated.

∘ ∘ ◦●◌ ∘ ∘

That evening everyone again gathered at Lawson's place. Mollie refused to talk about the dream and didn't want anyone else mentioning it.

Sham slowly approached the young girl. "Mollie, my boss, Cassidy, would like to meet you. She's really nice; I think you'll like her."

"My parents only gave Gren permission to wander," Mollie said. She turned her attention back to the toy in her hands.

"Not to wander," Sham assured her. "Cassidy just wants to talk. I really think that she can help."

Mollie looked at her partner, then back at Sham. "Can Winnie come too?"

Sham nodded. "Winnie can come too."

Mollie bit her lip in thought. "Okay." Once again, she turned her attention to her toy.

Sham walked back to where the rest of his friends were seated, taking the opportunity to poke Calli as he passed her.

Chapter Seven

Two rotations later Sham, Titus, Mollie, Winnie and Gren gathered in Cassidy's office. Gren had never met her before. She had heard a few not-so-kind things about Cassidy's practice from Haas, but she and Lawson had agreed not to tell Sham and Titus. Although Gren tried not to form opinions on people based on appearance, she could see immediately why Haas didn't like her. Cassidy's curly brown hair didn't seem to know which direction it wanted to go, her clothes were a bit on the wild side, and she seemed to be somewhat scatterbrained. The dark office was a mess, and the incense made Gren want to sneeze. The entire atmosphere was almost the opposite of Haas' practice, where everything shined with what he called "the utmost professionalism". Still, Gren was very impressed with the woman. She had a way of putting the children at ease. Mollie was even laughing, which was something that she hadn't done since her dream about Haas.

Instead of inquiring directly about the dreams that she had been experiencing, Cassidy asked a series of questions. "What's your favorite color?" was the latest.

"Blue," Mollie answered.

"Mine too! Dark or light, or kind of in between?"

"Kind of in between," Mollie said. "Leaning more towards dark I guess."

"Mine too!" Cassidy repeated. "How about this one...which do you prefer, sweet or salty?"

"Sweet," Mollie said.

"Me too." It was obvious that Cassidy was trying to gain Mollie's trust. "That's what most kids answer when I ask them that question. Okay, how about this. I'll tell you a story about something that happened to me, and then you tell me a story about your life. Sound good?"

Mollie nodded nervously.

Cassidy took a deep breath. "When I was a little bit younger than you are, I was getting ready to attend the Learning Center. It was a few rotations after we found out my placement and my parents were so proud! They decided that they were going to throw me a party. They planned it for probably a full lunar cycle. They invited all of their friends, all of my friends, all of my relatives, and I think even a few people that they couldn't stand, just because they wanted to brag about my placement." Cassidy laughed. "Anyway, the rotation of the party it rained and it rained and it rained. I thought that it was going to be a total waste. Our dwelling wasn't all that big and with everyone that we knew coming, no one would have enough room to breathe! But a couple of units before the guests were to arrive it stopped raining and the sky cleared up. My mom was so happy. Quickly we set things up outside, we finished just in time. It was a beautiful, clear evening. The party was going really well until my parents asked me to give a speech. I didn't have anything prepared—I had no idea that they were going to do that to me. I stood up on a chair so that everyone could see me. Problem was that the chair had been outside during the rain and it was wet. As soon as everyone was looking at me I slipped, fell off the chair and directly into a mud puddle! Everyone laughed. I was so embarrassed that I ran into the house and refused to come out again. The only person that I would even speak to for the rest of the party was a girl who lived nearby. She was my best friend. Sometimes it's really nice to have a good friend." Cassidy reached up to her head and grabbed one of her many curls. She laughed. "Imagine this hair, dripping with mud. It was so embarrassing at the time, but now I see the humor in it." She smiled. "Okay, Mollie, it's your turn."

"I don't know what to tell you about," Mollie said.

Cassidy continued to smile. "It could be anything. I know. Why don't you tell me about when you found out that you had been accepted to the Culinary Institute? That's such a prestigious school. How did your parents react?"

"My mom was really happy," Mollie started. "My dad..." She stopped.

Cassidy leaned slightly closer. "How did your dad react, Mollie? You can tell us, you're among friends."

"My dad was happy too, I guess. He just has a weird way of showing it. He keeps telling me that I need to study hard and do well, because I'm his chance at a better life. He's always saying that he hates his job and that once I'm a famous chef I can support him, instead of the other was around."

"How does that make you feel?" Cassidy asked.

"Like I need to be the best. But I'm not the best. I'm doing okay at school but I'm not at the top of the class. Dad is pretty mad at me about that, he says I need to try harder."

"Tell me about your mom," Cassidy said. "Are you and she close?"

Mollie perked up. "Yes! I love my mother so much. She tells

me to just try my hardest, and that will be enough."

"What do your parents think about the dreams that you've been having?" It was the first time that Cassidy had mentioned the subject.

"Mom is worried because she knows that I don't like it. Dad, well, I think he's scared that someone important will find out about them and that I'll get kicked out of school. That's why they only want Gren to wander. Winnie told Mom that she thought Gren could help. Dad doesn't even know why I'm here. He thinks I'm spending the break in the city, visiting restaurants and stuff. Which we are doing, so it's not like I'm lying to him."

"Mollie, if you don't mind, I'd like to talk to Gren alone for a couple of hundreds," Cassidy said. "Since she's the only one with permission to wander, I'm going to give her some tips."

"Okay," Mollie said.

Everyone else left, leaving Gren and Cassidy alone in the office. "It's definitely brought on by stress," Cassidy said. "Whether her father means it or not, Mollie believes that *his* entire future rests on *her* shoulders. Do you know how she's really doing in school?"

"From what Winnie has told me they're both near the top of the class," Gren said, "but there are a couple of partnerships that are slightly ahead of them."

"Poor girl," Cassidy said. "That's an awful lot of weight for her young shoulders. My advice is this; wander her dreams all you can. Not just the premonitions and not just nightmares. Constantly reassure her that her father loves her, but that his future doesn't depend on her doing well. She should be studying for her own future, not his. Let her know that she's doing well and that everyone is proud of her. She needs lots of positive reassurance. I don't know if that will make the premonitions stop, but if she feels less pressure they might subside somewhat. I'll keep looking; see if I can find out any more information on Premonition Dreaming. It's not a well-documented subject, most Dream Wanderers will deny that it's even possible. But I'll keep digging, and I'll let you know what I find out." Cassidy stood and motioned towards the door.

Gren reached out and shook Cassidy's hand. "Thank you for your help."

"You're most welcome. Keep me informed."

∘ ∘ ● ◐ ∘ ∘

Gren enjoyed having a few rotations off. She and Lawson, along with Calli and Tayo, took Winnie and Mollie all over the city. They visited museums, parks, and several more restaurants. Gren couldn't help but notice that Winnie was more interested in the restaurants than Mollie was. They spent their evenings with the guys, with Calli usually teasing Sham about what a great rotation they had enjoyed while he and Titus were working. Gren spent some time each rotation reading the books that they had borrowed from Cassidy. She also wandered each night. It was strange wandering her sister's dreams, but somehow she felt as if she was getting to know Winnie better through them. Gren wandered Mollie as well, reassuring her as Cassidy had suggested. Mollie's dreams were calm, almost boring. There had been no more premonitions since the dream about Haas.

∘ ∘ ● ◐ ∘ ∘

Ten rotations after his accident, Haas called all his workers into the office. He was out of the Medical Center but having a hard time getting around. Gren and Lawson arrived a few hundreds early. They took seats towards the back of the room. Haas' two Associate Wanderers sat in the front, the other employees filled in the rest of the seats. Haas entered. He was in a wheelchair, pushed by a tired-looking woman.

"That's his wife," Gren whispered to Lawson.

"How do you know?" Lawson asked. They had never met Haas' wife or even seen her picture.

"I recognize her from Mollie's dream."

There were other murmurs with Haas' entrance. Apparently, not everyone had visited him while he was in the Medical Center. He looked quite a bit better than when Gren and Lawson had stopped by. The bruising on his face had lessened and the cuts were no longer noticeable.

"Enough!" Haas' voice still bellowed. "I look dreadful, I know. However, more important than the way that I look is getting this practice up and running like it should be. Starting tomorrow, my Associate Wanderers will be practicing again. They'll be taking some of the easier cases. Aribella will be in charge."

The other associate stood up. "Sir," he said slowly, "I thought that you and I had agreed that—"

Haas wouldn't let him finish. "Sit down, Thaddeus. You *assumed* that I agreed with you. I never did. Aribella has much more experience and a better rapport with the clients. *She* will be in charge until my return."

"But Sir…"

"Thaddeus, just leave," Haas ordered. "Come back tomorrow when your attitude is better. I need my people to work together as a team, not argue about my decisions."

Thaddeus remained where he was, not moving.

"Go!"

After a micro Thaddeus stormed out of the room.

Haas looked at those remaining, sending a cold chill down several spines. "Now if there are no more interruptions...my reception staff has been in contact with all of our clients. Some are willing to see an Associate Wanderer; others have decided to wait for my return. Unfortunately, we've lost a few, but I guess that's to be expected. I will personally be returning in 12 rotations. The Medical Workers have assured me that I will be on crutches by then, and most of the other obvious signs of my accident should be gone. Taking this time off was a difficult decision for me, but in the long run, I decided that it was best for the children. Having them see their Wanderer look like something from one of their nightmares would only heighten their apprehension, and it could also avert their attention from what was really bothering them."

Haas' last statement surprised Gren. He had spoken it with compassion for the children. Until that micro Gren had assumed that he was in it only for the money.

"So," Haas continued, "whatever you need to do to get ready for tomorrow, go do it. I want to see the apprentices in my office in half a unit."

⋅ ⋅ ●●● ⋅ ⋅

Half a unit later Gren and Lawson sat in their usual places. Haas still looked sternly at them, but the wheelchair caused him to be slightly further away than normal. His wife stood behind them. "Gren," he began, "what have you been doing with your unexpected leave?"

"I've been doing as you asked, Sir," Gren replied. "I'm getting in plenty of practice. I've been wandering my sister and her friend every night."

"Good. How long will they be here?"

"The rest of the lunar cycle."

Haas paused in thought. "So they leave a few rotations after I return. I was going to have you both come in and work in the simulator, but I've changed my mind. I will allow you both to take the next 12 rotations off, as long as you continue to practice." He stared at Gren. "I expect to see a significant improvement."

"Yes, Sir."

Haas waved his hand. "You're both dismissed. You can go home, with everyone else preparing for tomorrow, if you stay here you'll only be in the way."

∘ ∘ ⦾●◉● ∘ ∘

"In the way?" Gren and Lawson were walking back towards her dwelling. "What does he think we're going to do? I mean, they're just getting ready to start up again tomorrow, it's not like we're going to run up and down the hallways screaming, or try to delete computer files! In the way…"

Lawson smiled. "It's no big deal. It's just Haas being Haas. Hey, at least we got off better than Thaddeus did. Imagine being put in your place like that in front of everybody…"

"Unfortunately I *can* imagine it, the way Haas acts sometimes."

"Gren!" a voice called from behind.

Gren turned. She had recognized Calli's voice. Calli, Tayo and Mollie were all running towards her. Something was wrong. "Where's Winnie?"

"Winnie has disappeared," Calli said, trying to catch her breath. "We were in the park. One hundred she was with us and the next…she was just gone. We've been looking for her for over a unit. I didn't know what else to do, so we came here."

"Come on." Gren ran towards the park. Her sister couldn't be missing. She just couldn't.

Chapter Eight

G ren and Lawson combed the park, looking for some sign of Winnie. Callie, Tayo and Mollie were there as well, reporting to the System Workers. "We were sitting over here." Calli pointed. "Mollie and Winnie were within our sight. They were rolling down the hill, just playing. There was nothing out of the ordinary at all."

"They came over to us and Winnie said that she needed to use the necessary room," Tayo added. She pointed as well, towards a small shelter. "Over there. We could still see Mollie, because she waited outside."

One of the System Workers, a young woman, squatted down to Mollie's level. "Remember, honey, this isn't your fault. Is there anything else that you can tell us?"

Mollie wiped the tears from her eyes. "Just that when Winnie was taking a long time I went in and called her name, but she didn't answer. I looked for her, but couldn't find her. That's when..." Mollie looked away, embarrassed.

The System Worker turned her attention towards Calli. "What happened?"

"Mollie screamed, and we came running."

A second System Worker finished his notes. "We'll search, of course. And the girl's parents will need to be notified."

"That's not possible." Gren had just approached the group

to see if there was anything new. Lawson was at her side. "Our parents are on an extended vacation. Since Winnie was spending her break with me, they decided to take the trip of their dreams. They're out of reach." Gren put her head down and started to cry. "They trusted me…"

Lawson put an arm around Gren's shoulder. "We'll find her, Gren. The whole group is back together. We can accomplish anything, remember?"

° ° ●●● ° °

Some of the System Workers searched the park, while the rest concentrated on the shelter that contained the necessary room. There were two entrances, the one that Winnie had used and another on the other side. Behind the second entrance was an area for glidemobile parking. The System Workers concluded that if someone had grabbed Winnie from the shelter, they could have been long gone before anyone even noticed that she was missing.

Even though it seemed pointless, Gren and Calli continued to call out Winnie's name. Tayo sat on a bench with Mollie. Lawson was no longer with them, but he returned less than a unit later with Sham, Titus and Cassidy. Lawson headed straight for Gren, while Sham and Titus went to search in a different part of the park.

Cassidy sat down on the bench next to Mollie. "Mind if I sit here?"

Mollie shook her head but didn't say anything.

Tayo had a feeling that Mollie and Cassidy needed to talk in private. "I'm going to stretch my legs," she said. "I'll be over there if you need me."

Cassidy put an arm around Mollie's shoulder. "This isn't

your fault."

"That's what the System Workers keep saying," Mollie replied. "That doesn't make it true."

"It is true." Cassidy squeezed a little bit tighter. "You had no way of knowing that something like this would happen. How have you been doing, otherwise? Have you been having a good visit?"

Mollie wiped her eyes. "Yeah. It's been a lot of fun. I love watching Winnie and Gren together. That's what siblings *should* be like."

"Do you have any brothers or sisters?" Cassidy asked.

Mollie nodded. "I have a brother who is two orbits older than I am. He's not very nice. He found out about my dreams, and he likes to tease me about them."

"Where does he go to school?"

"He didn't make it into any of the specialized schools, so he just attends locally. I was glad that I didn't have to spend the break at home, because he teases me about my dreams."

Since Mollie had mentioned the dreams twice Cassidy decided to ask her about them. "Have you had any more of those dreams since the last time we talked?"

Mollie shook her head. "I've been dreaming a lot, but not the type that come true."

"What have you been dreaming about?"

"I can't remember a lot of them. But what I do remember is mostly just normal stuff. Playing with Winnie, she's been in all of them. Just fooling around and having fun." Mollie wiped a few more tears from her eyes.

Cassidy patted Mollie's shoulder. "You really like Winnie, don't you."

Mollie nodded again. "She's the only real friend that I have. That I've ever had." Mollie pulled away and buried her head in her hands. She sobbed openly. "And I let her down."

"Why do you think that?" Cassidy was sure of the answer.

"Because my dreams tell the future! I should have known that this was going to happen. I should have been able to warn her. Instead, I decided that I want to get rid of the dreams. I should have tried to let them happen."

Cassidy sighed. "Mollie, you know very well that you don't have control over what you dream. Even if you did, I don't think that your mind would ever have allowed the possibility of Winnie disappearing. You can't blame yourself, not for any of it. Wherever Winnie is, I'm sure she's unharmed. She's a smart girl, and from what I hear she's very resourceful."

"She's been kidnapped, in a city that she doesn't know very well. What is she going to do without me?" Mollie cried harder. "What am I going to do without her?"

Cassidy placed her arms around the child, who welcomed the embrace. Mollie wept as if the tears would never stop.

∘ ∘ ◦ ● ◦ ∘ ∘

After searching for several units without the slightest clue, everyone decided that the group should split up. Gren headed back to her place, in case Winnie made her way there. Lawson and Mollie accompanied her. Sham and Titus also went home, since Winnie also knew how to get their dwelling as well. Calli and Tayo continued to search the park long after dark. Eventually they gave up and went back to Gren's. Although everyone tried to keep the mood light for Mollie and Gren's sakes, it was a solemn group.

Gren looked at the timekeeper on her wall. "Lawson, you

need to get going. There are only ten hundreds until curfew."

"Who cares about that?" Lawson asked. "My best friend needs me. I'd be more than happy to sleep on the floor or on a chair..."

"Thanks, but rules are rules. This is a female-only building, and the last thing I need right now is to be kicked out. Besides..." Gren walked Lawson to the door and motioned towards the outside.

Knowing Gren as well as he did, Lawson noticed her hint. "Good night everyone. I'll see you in the morning." He opened the door and closed it again when he and Gren were on the other side. "Besides what?"

"Besides, I want to see if I can get Mollie to go to sleep," Gren whispered. "Cassidy says that her premonitions are brought on by stress. Maybe she'll have one of the dreams tonight and we'll get a clue as to where Winnie is and why they took her."

"Do you think that will really happen?"

"It's a long shot," Gren said, "but it's the only thing that I can think of. It's better than doing nothing."

Lawson stared at Gren. "And if you find out any information, you'll tell the System Workers, right?"

Gren rolled her eyes. "Sure, Lawson. I'll tell them everything, and exactly how we found out. Not only would they not believe me, but then more people would find out what's going on with Mollie. I don't think that's what her parents had in mind when they sent her to me. No, if I find out anything, it's up to *us* to find my sister."

Lawson smiled, hoping to reassure his friend. "Yeah, we're pretty good in a crisis."

· ○ ○●◗○ ○ ·

Back inside, Gren yawned and stretched. "I don't think it's going to do Winnie any good for all of us to wear ourselves out. Let's go to bed. Mollie, if you'd like, I'll stay out here with you. I'm sure you probably don't want to be alone."

"Yes, please," Mollie said.

A few hundreds later, everyone was in bed and the lights were all out. Mollie buried her head in the pillow and cried herself to sleep.

Gren stayed awake, waiting.

· ○ ○●◗○ ○ ·

Winnie stood by the closed door, her ear right up against it. She was unharmed. She appeared to be listening hard. The morning light was starting to peek into the small, barren room.

"So now that we have her, what are we going to do with her?" a muffled male voice said.

"Give her a couple of rotations," a second man replied. "Let her get used to her surroundings. She'll start dreaming."

"And what if she doesn't?"

"I'll steal some tonic from work." The second man laughed. "My boss is such an idiot that it will never even be missed. I read all about it, certain sleep tonics will make the premonitions start."

"I still don't understand your plan," the first man said.

The second man sighed. "Wouldn't you like to know the future? We get her to dream about it, give away a couple of freebies to very rich, very superstitious clients, and then get them to pay us for more. We'll be rich ourselves before too long. I tell you, Mollie is going to make us more money than you could ever dream of. Dream of. Get it?" He laughed at his own joke.

"I sure hope so," the first man said. "We could end up in the Labor Camps for kidnapping...you think she's hungry? Should I bring her something?"

Winnie quickly stepped away from the door and lay down on the cot provided for her. "They think I'm Mollie," Winnie whispered to herself.

Chapter Nine

Winnie had no idea how she had come to be in the tiny room. She remembered being at the park with Calli and Tayo. She and Mollie went to the small shelter that contained the necessary room. Mollie had waited outside. The next thing Winnie knew, something had been placed over her mouth and nose and everything went black. When she woke up, she was in a small, barren room. She was lying on a cot. Something in the back of her mind told her not to cry out. It was dark, but there was a small amount of light starting to peek through a window. Winnie quietly stood up and looked outside. All she could see were trees. She listened carefully, there were two voices coming through the door. She tiptoed to the door and, trying not to make any noise, placed her ear as close as possible. The thickness of the door distorted the voices but she could still make them out.

"So now that we have her, what are we going to do with her?" a male voice said.

"Give her a couple of rotations," a second man replied. "Let her get used to her surroundings. She'll start dreaming."

"And what if she doesn't?"

"I'll steal some tonic from work." The second man laughed. "My boss is such an idiot that it will never even be missed. I read all about it, certain sleep tonics will make the premonitions start."

"I still don't understand your plan," the first man said.

The second man sighed. "Wouldn't you like to know the future? We get her to dream about it, give away a couple of freebies to very rich, very superstitious clients, and then get them to pay us for more. We'll be rich ourselves before too long. I tell you, Mollie is going to make us more money than you could ever dream of. Dream of. Get it?" He laughed again.

"I sure hope so," the first man said. "We could end up in the Labor Camps for kidnapping…you think she's hungry? Should I bring her something?"

Fearing that the men were about to enter, Winnie quickly stepped away from the door and lay back down on the cot. "They think I'm Mollie," she whispered to herself. She thought fast. Obviously, these two men had somehow found out about Mollie's dreams. It didn't really matter how they had found out, all that was important was what they planned on doing. As Winnie stayed still in the dim light, she was surprised that she wasn't scared. She needed to play along until they made a mistake. She heard a sound, someone fiddling with the door.

"Hey, kid, you awake?" A man entered, carrying a tray of food.

Winnie sat up. She pretended to be frightened, knowing that they would expect her to be. She had a hard time not laughing at the mask the man wore over his face. It was supposed to look like a large, fierce animal. The animal's nose protruded from the front of the mask with sharp, white teeth. "Where—where am I?"

"That doesn't matter," the man replied. The mask somewhat muffled his voice. "You hungry?"

Winnie nodded. "A little bit."

The man set the tray on the bed next to her. He seemed offended that Winnie moved slightly away. "Don't be scared, kid. I'm not going to hurt you."

Winnie recognized his voice as the first man that she had heard speaking. "I'm…I'm…my name is Mollie."

"Nice to meet you, Mollie, although I already knew your name."

"What's…what's your name?"

The man laughed. "I'm not going to tell you my name, for reasons that I would think are obvious. But you can call me…how about you call me 'Number One'? Or just 'One' for short."

Winnie needed to suppress another laugh. What a *stupid* sounding moniker! 'One' obviously wasn't the brains of whatever they were planning. "What…what do you want from me, One?"

"I just want you to be comfortable," One replied. We're not going to hurt you, I promise. There's a necessary room through that door," he pointed, "you know, in case you need it."

"I'm going to head out for work," a voice called from the other room. "You need anything?"

"No, I've got things under control," One called back. "Mollie and I will be fine."

"Okay, see you later." There was the sound of a door slamming shut.

"Who…who was that?" Winnie asked.

"That, Mollie, was Number Two."

○ ○ ○◉◑ ○ ○

Winnie sat on the edge of the small bed and concentrated. She had already put a couple of facts together. She knew that

Number One was the more compassionate of the two men. He had brought her food and kept checking to make sure that she didn't need anything. She couldn't help but thinking how badly he needed a few cooking lessons! She knew that she should try to interact with him; maybe he would give her some useful information.

There was very little that she knew about Number Two. He had yet to return from work. Work. The word stuck in Winnie's brain. She thought back to the conversation that she had overheard through the door. Number Two had mentioned dreaming, sleep tonic and premonitions. He must be a Dream Wanderer! But wandering was a lucrative career, why go to all the trouble of kidnapping someone for premonitions? How did he even find out about Mollie and her dreams? Outside of Gren and her friends, there was only one person locally who knew about Mollie's dreams...Cassidy. Was Cassidy somehow involved? And if so, why did they grab the wrong person?

Winnie took a deep breath and let it out slowly. All the information was useless unless she had some way to pass it on to Gren. If only Gren could somehow read her mind, hear her thoughts. There might be a way! Winnie remembered Gren telling her that she and Lawson would sometimes communicate by Lawson letting his mind wander, staying awake but entering a dream-like state. Winnie also knew that Gren could wander distances. Winnie lay back down and closed her eyes.

⋅ ∘ ◐● ◑ ∘ ⋅

Winnie pictured herself running through the park. Mollie was chasing her. Out of the corner of her eye, Winnie could see Calli and Tayo sitting under a tree, talking. Winnie remembered Gren telling her that Calli and Tayo hadn't always been so close, in fact, they used to fight all the time, but Winnie had a hard time believing that.

"Hey, Winnie, over here!"

Winnie ran to where Mollie had called her. It was nice to see her partner having such a good time. In the few lunar cycles since they had met, Winnie had seen Mollie serious, stern, worried, nervous, sad, and many other moods that didn't seem to suit a girl her age. It was rare that Mollie would laugh. Suddenly, it was as if Mollie was allowing herself to be a kid. She was relaxed and having fun! The dreams that Mollie hated so much had stopped, adding credence to the theory that stress caused them. Winnie was grateful to Gren that she was making her friend feel so at home, and hoped that it would just be the first of many breaks that they spent with her sister.

"Maybe next time we're here things will be better for Gren at work." It sounded like a strange thing for Mollie to say, until Winnie remembered that this was happening in her imagination. Maybe that was on her mind as well.

"They will. Gren can do anything." Winnie hoped that Gren was wandering; she wanted her sister to know how much she looked up to her.

"Come on, Winnie, over here." Mollie stood at the top of a small hill and started to roll down. She laughed as she went.

Winnie joined her. "This is fun!" They ran up the hill and rolled back down several times. "Mollie, I have to…" She pointed with her head towards the necessary room.

Mollie grabbed Winnie by the shoulders. "No, you can't go in there! There's a man wearing a really stupid mask. He'll grab you, put something over your face, and when you wake up you'll be in a small room somewhere. The only thing you'll be able to see out the dirty window will be a bunch of trees. You'll then hear two men. One of the men will stay behind with you, the other needs to go off to work. He's probably a Dream Wanderer, because you'll hear him mention stealing sleep tonic. He's got to be somehow connected to Cassidy, because no one else knows about my dreams. Winnie, they'll think you're me! You'll play along, of course, and try to get as much information as possible. Anything you find out you'll try to pass along to Gren, hoping that she's wandering."

"Gren?" Winnie asked with hope in her voice. "They think I'm Mollie. I'm playing along. Gren, this has got to be somehow related to Cassidy. No one else knows about Mollie's dreams. I don't think we should trust her, Gren." She paused. "Gren, are you there?"

There was no reply.

Chapter Ten

Sham and Titus both felt guilty about going to work the next morning, but they knew that there wasn't anything that they could do by just sitting at home. They left a note on their door; instructions on how to contact them on the off chance that Winnie showed up.

Cassidy greeted them as soon as they entered the office. "Any word?" She purposely didn't say too much, she knew that things needed to be kept as quiet as possible.

Sham shook his head. "No."

"I'm sure she's fine." Cassidy lowered her voice. "There's nothing to be gained by hurting a child."

Titus glanced at Sham. Cassidy's wording seemed a bit strange to him. Sham didn't seem to have noticed it. They followed Cassidy down the hall.

"I'm going to have you two observe today," Cassidy informed them. "Wandering when you're under a lot of stress isn't a good idea."

"We can handle it," Sham said.

"I'm sure you think you can," Cassidy replied sternly, "but this is *my* practice, and *my* reputation is on the line. Neither of you have had enough practice on actual clients and I don't have the time or the patience to babysit you today."

Sham almost stopped in his tracks. Cassidy had never

spoken to them like that before. "We don't need a babysitter—"

Although he was also surprised at the way that Cassidy had spoken to them, Titus put his hand on his friend's shoulder and squeezed it firmly. "Whatever you think is best."

"Good." Cassidy led them into one of the wandering rooms. Grey was already there. He looked tired and even more miserable than usual. "Grey will be doing the wandering, I want the two of you to observe."

Sham stood there for several micros, speechless. "We have to observe…him?" he asked at last.

Grey sat there and smiled. Upon hearing that his rivals would be observing him, his usually sullen mood picked up quite a bit.

"It will be fine," Titus said to Sham, his voice just above a whisper. He absentmindedly rubbed his jaw where Grey had punched him. It seemed like it had been orbits ago.

"I'm going to get the child ready," Cassidy said. She pulled back a curtain, revealing a window. The child would soon be on the other side. "Remember, Grey, you wander. Sham, Titus, you observe. Silently." She left the room.

As soon as the door was closed, Grey started to laugh. "So, the high and mighty Sham has to observe poor, pitiful Grey. Think you'll be able to handle it?"

"Sure," Sham replied. "We'll get a great lesson—in how *not* to wander."

"Let's just see if you can keep up with me."

"Keep up?" Sham laughed. "I think the only reason that Cassidy even lets you wander is because you *bore* the nightmares away from the kids."

"Why you—" Grey stood up and took a step towards Sham.

Titus stepped in between them, knowing that he was yet again placing himself in danger. "I know you two hate each other, but *think about the child*! Some poor kid is coming in here with dreams bad enough that his parents think they should be wandered, and you two are turning it into a competition! This is *definitely* against our oath." He took the seat in the middle, facing the window.

"He's right," Sham said. "We've got to think about the kid. He comes first."

"She," Grey corrected. "The client is a girl."

Cassidy appeared through the window. She was with a girl who was probably close to Winnie's age. Titus glanced at Sham, who didn't seem to notice. The girl's mother took a seat next to the bed. Cassidy handed the girl a cup, she drank it, lay down on the bed and took her mother's hand.

Grey stretched and yawned. "Time to make this kid's good dreams come true."

Dreams come true. Sham stared at Grey, a theory growing in his mind. It couldn't be.

＊ ＊ ＊ ● ○ ＊ ＊

After work, Sham and Titus ran to Gren's building. Gren folded up the extra cots and stuck them in the bedroom so that there would be enough room for everyone to fit. She and Lawson had been out most of the rotation, looking for Winnie in any place that they could think of. Tayo had stayed behind in case she returned. Calli had taken Mollie out for a little while, but it hadn't helped. The poor child was blaming herself.

"I have a theory," Sham started just micros after Gren had opened the door. He glanced around. Calli, Tayo and Mollie all sat on the floor. Lawson was sitting on a small sofa. Gren took the only open seat next to him. Titus immediately plopped down on the floor next to Calli. She had asked him a couple of rotations earlier to help keep some distance between herself and Sham, his constant poking was no longer amusing. "You sure you don't want to take this over to our place? There's a lot more room."

"Just sit down and tell us your theory," Lawson said.

"I think that Grey had something to do with Winnie's disappearance."

"Grey?" everyone but Mollie said in unison. Since Grey had attended the Learning Center they all knew who he was, although they hadn't had much contact with him since he was older than they were. He had always come across as a bit of a loner.

"Sham, you're crazy," Titus said. "This is *Grey* you're talking about. Grey! The guy isn't smart enough to pull something like this off, and he certainly doesn't have the ambition. Think about it."

"I don't know," Sham said. "Think of how he was acting today. Tired and irritable."

"Grey is always tired and irritable."

"He was even more so today. Come on, Titus, you saw him. He was ready to pick a fight before he started wandering. It took nothing to set him off! You even had to remind him of the oath. Isn't that how someone acts when they haven't had any sleep?"

Titus stared straight ahead, thinking. "Grey wasn't at work when Winnie was grabbed. He claimed he was sick."

"Wait a hundred," Lawson said. "I'll admit I barely know the guy, but why would Grey want to kidnap Winnie? It just doesn't make sense."

"He thinks she's me," Mollie said quietly.

"Huh?" The news surprised Sham.

"Mollie had another premonition last night," Gren said to Sham. "Sorry, I guess I forgot to tell you and Titus. We know that Winnie isn't hurt. She could hear two male voices; one of them is most likely a Wanderer. He said something about having to go to work. They were talking about Mollie's dreams, making money by knowing the future. They called her 'Mollie'. Fortunately Winnie realized that they think she's Mollie, I'm sure she'll play along."

"Wait a hundred," Lawson said again. "This still doesn't mean that it's Grey. I mean, how would he even know about Mollie's dreams?"

"I don't know," Sham said, slightly let down.

"I do!" Titus said. "We were talking about this with Cassidy at work! Grey's not above eavesdropping, and it's not like Cassidy's doors are soundproof. He knew we were excited about something, listened in, and then..." Titus took a breath. "Sham, Grey was there when Cassidy gave us the books! I bet he looked through them when we brought them back, saw the picture of Purcella, and assumed that Winnie was the one having the dreams."

"Who's Purcella?" Mollie asked.

"She's a girl who had the same type of dreams that you do," Calli explained. "A long time ago. Her picture was in one of the books that Cassidy gave us. She looked a lot like Winnie."

"Why didn't you show us?"

"Because I thought it might bother Winnie," Gren explained. "The resemblance was so strong that it was almost creepy." She purposely left out the part about Purcella's suicide.

"Okay, back to Grey," Tayo said. "I still don't see what he hopes to accomplish."

Sham sighed. "Cassidy told us that Grey is always looking for the quick and easy way. Maybe he thinks he found it."

"'We'll be rich ourselves before too long.'" Gren added. "That's what someone said in Mollie's dream. Something about giving rich people a few freebies and then making money off of them."

"Cassidy also told us that with the right combination of tonics the dreams could happen more frequently," Titus said. "Grey must have heard that too."

"I want to do it," Mollie said quietly.

"Do what?" Gren asked.

"Take the tonics to make the dreams happen."

Gren was shocked; the idea hadn't even crossed her mind. "No! Mollie, it's one thing if you have a dream on your own, but I'm not going to make them happen. In fact, maybe you should spend the rest of your break at home with your family."

Mollie shook her head. "No, I'm not going anywhere. Winnie is missing because of me, and I can help you find her. We know that she's not hurt because of my dream last night."

Calli stroked Mollie's hair. "Gren's just thinking about what's best for you."

"What's best for me is finding Winnie."

Gren nodded. "Okay, Mollie, you can stay—but no tonic. If we're going to find out any information I want it to happen on its own."

"But if it will help—"

"Dreams with tonic are easier to manipulate anyway," Lawson explained. "You want to keep your dreams as pure as possible. Plus Gren is right. We're not going to experiment on you, Mollie. We wouldn't even know what the right mixture would be. It's not like they taught a class on this at the Learning Center. Premonition Dreaming isn't even supposed to exist."

Tayo decided that the subject needed to be changed. "Gren, how much does Winnie know about wandering? And last orbit?"

"We're not allowed to talk about that," Gren quickly reminded her. "But she knows a little bit about wandering." Gren grew excited. "I told her how Lawson is good at letting his mind wander and putting himself into a dreamlike state and I can wander that. She also knows that it's possible to wander distances. Maybe we can take turns..."

"We don't have permission from your parents to wander Winnie's dreams," Titus reminded Gren. "She's a minor, it's against the oath."

"Our parents are away, unreachable," Gren said quickly. "They put me in charge of Winnie, and as her temporary guardian I give all of you permission to try to wander her."

"I can't wander distances," Calli said.

Gren stared at her friend. "Neither could I, until I had to. It's going to be hard, picking up one dream when we don't even know where to look, but we have to try."

"I will," Tayo said. The rest of the room agreed.

"Maybe I'll have another dream tonight," Mollie added.

"Sham and I will try to find out all we can about Grey," Titus said. "His friends, his hangouts, things like that."

Sham suppressed a laugh. "If Grey *has* any friends."

Titus ignored Sham and continued. "Maybe we'll get some sort of hint as to where he would be able to stash Winnie."

"Good idea." Gren was grateful to have something to do besides look for nonexistent clues. "What we need to do is set up a schedule on who will try to wander and when..."

As Gren organized, Titus leaned over to Sham. "I'm glad you picked up on the clues about Grey," he whispered, "because I was scared that somehow Cassidy was involved."

Chapter Eleven

"And then you just add a little bit of seasoning," Winnie said as she stirred something on a stove.

Number One stood next to her. He appeared to be watching what she was doing, but it was hard to tell for sure because he was wearing a mask. "How do you know when you've added enough?"

Winnie laughed. "You taste it, silly! Remember to add it slowly, though, because 'you can always add more, but you can't take away'. That's one of the first rules they taught us at school." Winnie picked up another spoon and took out some of the contents of the pot. She tried it. "It's pretty good—but it's missing something. Remember, I'm first orbit, I have a long way to go." She grabbed another spoon and scooped out some more. "Here, you try it."

"Sure, Mollie, get me to take off my mask."

Winnie shook her head no. "I wasn't trying to, I promise. I'll...I'll turn around until you say otherwise. I just wanted you to try it."

One laughed. "I'm just teasing you, Mollie. But your turning around isn't a bad idea."

Winnie turned so that her back was facing One. She glanced around the small room. They were in a cabin of some type. There were a couple of dirty windows; from where she was standing all that was visible through them were trees.

"Okay," One said.

"What did you think?" Winnie asked as she faced him again.

One laughed again. "I think that you should do all the cooking around here."

The door to the cabin opened. "Holy splarsh!" It closed again.

Winnie turned and looked in the direction of the door. All she saw was a man from the back. He was taller than One, and had collar length dark hair.

A micro later, the door opened again. The man returned, this time wearing a mask. "What's the kid doing in here?" The mask distorted his voice even more than One's did. The man was carrying something.

One faced his partner. "Look, Two, you leave us here alone all rotation, I'm not going to keep her locked up by herself. And she has a name."

"I made you the evening meal," Winnie said quietly.

"Put her back," Two ordered.

Without being asked, Winnie walked back to her small room.

"Sorry about him," One whispered. He closed the door and locked it behind him.

Winnie put her ear to the door and tried to listen. "And how come I have to be Number Two? This whole thing was my idea!"

∘ ∘ ◉ ◉ ∘ ∘ ∘

"Did it happen again?" Mollie sat excitedly on the bed.

Gren was next to her, frantically writing things down. "Yeah, Mollie, you did great. Do you remember any of it?"

"A couple of little bits and pieces are still there," Mollie replied. "I can hear Winnie laughing, that's a good sign, right?"

"That's a very good sign." Gren finished what she was writing and put the paper down. "Winnie isn't hurt, and she isn't scared, we know that much. They still don't know that they have the wrong person, and Winnie seems to be playing along."

"What happens when they find out that they don't have me?"

Gren hadn't even thought of that. "Mollie, promise me that you won't go anywhere without one of us. We don't want to lose you too. There's strength in numbers. It looks like there are only two of them, if you're always with someone else, you'll be fine."

Mollie nodded. "I promise."

Gren smiled slightly. She was still extremely worried about her sister, but proud at the same time. Winnie was obviously very smart and playing along with whatever the two men were planning. She also knew from the first dream that the two men didn't expect any premonitions for a few rotations. By then, Winnie would be back, and the two men in the Labor Camp.

"Did you learn anything helpful?" Mollie asked. "Besides that Winnie was laughing?"

Gren picked up her notes. She stared at what she had written, although the picture was still fresh in her mind. She had seen the back of Two's head. His hair was the same color and length as Grey's hair. From the glimpse that she had been given he appeared also to be about the same height and build. Maybe Sham's theory was true. "She seems to be befriending one of the men. You know Winnie, her personality is infectious. Getting him to like her can only work her to advantage."

"What about the other man?" Mollie asked.

Gren paused. If it *was* Grey then she knew he didn't make friends easily. From what she had witnessed in the dream, the second man wasn't overly sociable. "He wasn't in your dream for very long."

The answer seemed to satisfy Mollie. "So what do we do now?"

"We get some sleep," Gren suggested. She waited until Mollie was comfortable, tucked her in, and gave her a kiss on the forehead. "We're going to be of no help to Winnie if we're all exhausted." Gren turned out the lights and closed her eyes. She knew that at that micro it was Lawson's turn to try to search for Winnie's dreams. She hoped that he was successful.

Chapter Twelve

The next morning Gren and Lawson headed to the Office of Records. They didn't really know what they were looking for, but it was better than doing nothing. Mollie stayed back at Gren's with Calli and Tayo, who were to take turns trying to reach out to Winnie.

"I'm sorry that I didn't have any luck last night," Lawson said. Calli had loaned them her glidemobile and he turned it on. "There's such a shady line. I mean, I found so many dreams out there, but I couldn't really enter any of them because it's wrong. So I peeked quickly, just long enough so that I could maybe see if it was Winnie."

"Things went better for us." As soon as the doors of the glidemobile closed, Gren told Lawson about Mollie's dream.

Lawson sighed with relief. "So we know she's okay."

"We know more than that. We know that she's befriended one of the men, which I'm sure can only work to her advantage. And when she looked out the window, there were a lot of trees. It's not much to go on but it's better than nothing."

"Do you think we should tell the System Workers?"

Gren almost laughed. "Tell them what? That we think that Winnie was snatched by a couple of guys wearing bad masks who are someplace where there are a lot of trees? That we learned this because Winnie's partner has been having premonition dreams, which, according to several reputable Wanderers *including Haas*, isn't even possible? Or that we believe that one of the people who took Winnie is Grey, because Sham said he was tired at work? Come on, Lawson, you know that we have to do this on our own."

"Yeah, I guess you're right."

"At least we know that we make a good team."

"That we do." Lawson pulled the glidemobile up in front of a large building. "Let me do the talking," he whispered as they approached it.

Once inside, Lawson walked up to the man at the desk. "We would like some information, please."

"This is the place for it," the man replied. He was wearing a security guard's uniform. "Ya got any paperwork?"

"Are you from Abacu?" Lawson asked with a smile.

"Yeah, so, what's it to ya?"

"I have a friend from Abacu," Lawson replied. "Perhaps you know him. His name is Roy."

The guard rolled his eyes. "Yeah, I know him. Of course I know him. I know every stinkin' person from Abacu on this side of Terra!"

Lawson was glad for some connection. "Isn't Roy a great guy?"

"Lawson," Gren whispered into her friend's ear, "he was being sarcastic."

"Oh."

"Ya got the paperwork or not?" the guard asked.

"What kind of paperwork would we need?" Gren asked sweetly.

"It depends on what kind of information ya need."

"We're looking for information on a friend," Gren said. "General background, family property holdings, that kind of thing."

"Well, if this person is a 'friend', then why don't ya just ask him? Or her. The Office of Records ain't here so that ya can go snoopin' around in other people's business."

"That's not our intention," Lawson said. "We just wanted to find out a few things—for a surprise party."

"Ya gonna invite me?" The guard laughed. "Go away, kids. Ya ain't gettin' nothin' from me without the proper paperwork."

"Thanks anyway." Gren pulled on Lawson's arm and they left the building. "I have an idea," she told her friend once they were outside. "There's someone else who might be able to help us."

· · ●●◐ · ·

It took a couple of units to get to the Learning Center. Neither of them had been back since their graduation. Since the school was on break, it was quieter than either of them had ever seen it. They parked Calli's glidemobile and headed towards the main building. Lawson tried to take Gren's hand but she pulled away.

"Sorry," Gren explained, "I know that we've graduated, but it still doesn't seem right."

"I will always hate that rule," Lawson said. He had struggled with the fact that he hadn't been allowed to have any physical contact with his partner the whole time they were students. "It's still haunting me, even after graduation."

"What if she's not here?" Gren asked, purposely changing the subject. "It's school break. What if she's gone?"

"Then we'll find someone else who knew him," Lawson replied. "The teachers and whole staff all live here. There's got to be at least one person who can give us something to go on."

They entered the building and walked to Ladinda's office. It was a path that they both knew all too well; they had made the same walk countless times, especially during their final orbit as students. Their partnership had almost been broken up and it seemed that they had spent nearly as much time in Ladinda's office as they had in class. Gren took a deep breath and knocked. She realized that she was shaking.

"Come in."

"Ladinda, Ma'am," Gren said slowly as she and Lawson entered the room, "we were hoping that we might have a hundred of your time."

"Gren! Lawson!" Ladinda stood up from behind her desk and approached them. She gave Gren a hug and then Lawson. "It's so good to see you both. Please, take a seat." They took their usual seats in front of the desk as Ladinda sat back down as well. "How is your apprenticeship going?"

Gren wasn't sure how to answer, but didn't really want to tell the whole truth. "We're learning a lot."

Seeing right through Gren's comment, Ladinda smiled. "Yes, Haas is a hard man to like sometimes. Very difficult to get along with. However, once he says you're ready, you'll be amongst the best Wanderers in the business. I heard about his accident. Is that what brings you here? Unexpected time off?"

Lawson sunk a little bit lower in his chair. He couldn't help feeling as if he was in trouble again. "Actually, Ma'am, we were wondering if you could tell us about a former student. He was an orbit ahead of us. His name is Grey."

"Sham and Titus are apprenticing in the same practice, and they're having a hard time getting along with him," Gren said quickly. She didn't want Ladinda to have too many questions. "We were thinking that if we found out more about him that maybe there would be some way for everyone to get along..."

If Ladinda didn't believe the story, she didn't let it show. "I can't give you personal information about a former student. As administrator that would be against my moral code. But if you take a stroll around the campus and run into one of your former teachers...Hutch, for example, well, there's nothing wrong with the three of you having a little chat." She glanced at something on her desk. "In fact, he's probably going to be in his classroom in a unit or so."

"Thank you, Ma'am," Gren said. She stood. "We've kept you long enough. It was really good seeing you again."

Ladinda walked them to the door. "Please, come back and visit! You will both always have a place here."

Gren took a step out into the hallway, stopped, and then turned back around. "Ladinda, Ma'am, do you believe that Premonition Dreaming is possible?"

Ladinda thought carefully before answering. "I've never seen a case of it but I've learned a lot over the orbits that I've been in this business. The most important thing that I've learned is not to dismiss any possibilities. Therefore, I'm not going to say that it's *not* possible. Why do you ask?"

"Just a conversation that a bunch of us were having," Gren said. "And once again, thank you for your time."

Since Gren and Lawson had some time before they would be able to see Hutch, they took a walk. Neither of them were surprised that they ended up by the lake. They had spent much of their time there when they were students. Whenever they were happy, sad, frustrated or bored, they ended up sitting beneath a favorite tree, looking out over the water. When Lawson had disappeared during their final orbit, the lake was the first place that Gren looked. It still showed up in their dreams.

Lawson sat down under "their" tree. "It's strange being back."

Gren sat next to him. "In some ways it feels like we never left." Hidden meaning filled her words.

Lawson understood. "I always hated that rule. I was hoping that one rotation Ladinda would explain it to us, but she never did."

"It's to build character," Gren said casually. "She gives her students one crazy rule, a big, almost impossible one that makes no sense, and if they can follow that...they can do just about anything they put their minds to."

"Did someone tell you that?"

"No," Gren replied. "But knowing Ladinda and the extremes she will go to—it just kind of makes sense. But it's not true. I can't do anything right lately. I can't even take care of my little sister for a lunar cycle while my parents are away." Gren put her head in her hands and started to cry.

Lawson put his arm around his former partner's shoulder. "Gren, we're going to find her. And you know that she's fine, you've seen her in Mollie's dreams. Knowing Winnie, she's just going to say that all of this was fun, a good lesson on life, and brag about how she got to do all the cooking."

Gren tried to pull away from Lawson. "We can't do this."

"Yes we can!" Lawson felt slightly guilty about raising his voice. "I'm sorry, Gren. But we don't go to school here anymore; we don't live under their rules. That was what bothered me the most, when I knew you needed a hug or a shoulder to cry on and I could only stand by and watch you hurt." Lawson paused and pulled Gren a little bit closer. "Did I ever tell you what happened that caused Hutch to recommend that we be split up?"

Gren shook her head.

The question had been to raise a little bit of courage, Lawson already knew that he had never told her. "Hutch wandered my dream. He manipulated it to get the information that he wanted from me. I told him that I'm in lo…"

Gren pulled away quickly and stood up. "Not now, Lawson. We can't have this conversation. The rules may be looser now that we're apprenticing but they're still there. And I can't concentrate on anything but finding Winnie."

"I'm sorry, I shouldn't have said anything."

It was Gren's turn to feel guilty. "Our time will come. Compared to all that we've been through already, two orbits as apprentices will seem like nothing. And you're right, we've graduated, we're not expected to follow Ladinda's rules anymore." She held out her hand and helped Lawson up. "Let's go find Hutch."

Hand in hand, they walked towards the classrooms.

∘ ∘ ●◐● ∘ ∘

Things were exactly as they remembered them. Hutch's desk was in the same place, there were a couple of chairs, and in the center of the room was the wandering table. "I don't miss that thing," Lawson commented.

"I don't miss the nightmares," Gren added. "Why is it that the tonic that we used the most as students is the one that produces the worst dreams?"

"To prepare you for practice," a voice said from behind them. "If you experience the dreams yourself *and* learn to wander them, it gives you better experience. No one hires a Dream Wanderer to make *good* dreams go away."

"Hutch!" Gren exclaimed. She hurried towards him and gave him a hug.

Lawson considered shaking hands but hugged their former teacher instead. "It's good to see you, Sir."

"I feel the same way. What brings you two back here?" Hutch sat down. Gren and Lawson took seats nearby.

"Calli's glidemobile," Lawson joked.

Gren rolled her eyes. "The man that we're apprenticing under had an accident and is taking some time off, and so we have some free time as well. We thought it would be fun to come back for a visit."

Hutch grinned. "I know you both very well. Coming back for a visit is good, and I'm glad you're here, but what's the real reason?"

Lawson decided to just come out and ask. "Do you remember Grey? He was an orbit older than we were. Sham and Titus are apprenticing with him, and they're having a hard time getting along. We thought that maybe if we found out something about him—"

"That you'd then have something that they could use against him?"

Gren looked horrified. "No, nothing like that. We thought that maybe we could help them find some common ground."

Hutch grinned again. "I'm just teasing, Gren. Yeah, I remember Grey. He was a bit of a loner. Lawson, you and he have something in common in that you both were orphaned."

"Really?" Lawson had always assumed that he had been the only student there without living parents.

"Different circumstances," Hutch continued. "He was in either Orange or Yellow orbit when his parents died. And he has a brother several orbits older who became his legal guardian. I never met his brother. He had finished the program before I started teaching here."

"His brother is a Dream Wanderer?" Gren asked.

"His brother attended school here," Hutch corrected. "Whether or not he became a Dream Wanderer I couldn't tell you. I don't even know his name."

Lawson didn't understand what Grey's brother had to do with anything. "What else can you tell us about Grey? What are his likes and dislikes? Or where, for example, would he spend his breaks? Did he just stay at home with his brother, or did they go somewhere special?"

Hutch knew that they weren't telling him something, but chose to ignore it. "I remember him mentioning that he and his brother had inherited a small cabin. They would spend his breaks there, because it wasn't too far from where his brother worked."

"Do you know where the cabin is?" Gren asked. She and Lawson glanced at each other, they were getting close.

"Somewhere near Lake Collins."

"That's got to be it!" Lawson exclaimed.

"That's got to be what?" Hutch asked.

Lawson looked embarrassed. "Um, that's got to be the type

of information we're looking for. Grey has a cabin near Lake Collins, and Sham loves spending time out in nature."

Hutch raised his eyebrows. "Sham and nature? Come on, you two, what are you really doing here?"

Gren decided to give Hutch a small amount of the truth. "Do you believe that dreams can come true?"

"Sometimes, but it's rare," Hutch replied. "What does that have to do with Grey?"

"I was wandering this young girl's dream," Gren explained, giving as few details as possible. "Grey was in it, even though she doesn't know him. There was a cabin in the woods. We were wondering if the place even existed."

"Then why didn't you just ask? Instead of making up with a story about Sham and nature?"

"They *are* having a hard time getting along," Lawson said. "Sham and Grey especially, although Titus doesn't like him either. It's affecting their work. Since I'm still rooming with them they're driving me crazy, complaining about him all the time."

Gren's eyes grew big, she had an idea. She stood up, hoping that Lawson would follow her lead. "We have to go. Calli's going to think that we stole her glidemobile. It's been great seeing you again, Sir."

"Stop by again soon," Hutch called after them as they took off out the door. "And tell Sham and Titus hello from me!" He chuckled slightly as they disappeared from sight.

○　○●○○　○

Gren didn't say another word until they were inside Calli's glidemobile. "Lawson, you're a genius."

"I know I am," he said. He paused. "What was my brilliant

idea this time?"

"Sham and Titus. We'll get them to befriend Grey, and then he'll slip up and give them information about where he took Winnie."

Lawson shook his head. "It's not going to happen. Gren, you don't live with them. I was serious when I said they drive me crazy with their complaints about him."

Gren's face fell. "So coming here was a total waste of time."

Lawson patted Gren's hand. "Not at all! I *do* have an idea, one that's worthy of your calling me a genius. I have some money saved up. We'll rent a cabin up by Lake Collins for a few rotations. We can search for Winnie; maybe you or Mollie will recognize something from her dreams. At least we'll be closer to where Grey has her. It will make it easier to try to wander. Once we can pinpoint her dreams, we'll be able to communicate with her, at least to some extent. We'll find her. And a few rotations at Lake Collins could do all of us some good."

Gren kissed Lawson on the cheek. "You *are* a genius after all."

Chapter Thirteen

It didn't take Winnie long to figure out that Number One wasn't going to hurt her. He seemed almost as bored as she was, he kept bringing her food. She wasn't as sure about Number Two. She hadn't had as much contact with him, he was gone most of the rotation, every rotation. Since she had heard him mention "work", she assumed that was where he would go. She had thought more about her theory that Cassidy was involved. It was still the only thing that made any sense to her. Maybe Cassidy was joined, and one of them was her husband, or maybe it was Cassidy's brother. Winnie remembered that Gren had once told her that the gift of wandering didn't usually run in families, but occasionally it would happen. She still didn't understand why they thought she was Mollie. Cassidy had met them both; she knew who had been having the premonition dreams.

The door opened, and Number One entered. He was carrying a tray. "I thought you might be hungry."

Winnie took the tray and took a bite of the food. Without meaning to, she made a face.

"Is it *that* bad?"

"Let's just say that it's obvious that you didn't study culinary arts." Winnie decided to take a chance. "I know I'm only first orbit, but I can help. Maybe give you a tip or two."

Number One shook his head. "I don't know…"

"Come on," Winnie pleaded. "I won't try anything, I promise. I'm just a kid, what could I do? And it might help pass the time. Please, One, I'm really bored."

One drummed his fingers against his mask. "Okay, but one wrong move and you're back in here."

"Deal."

∘ ∘ ◦●◦ ∘ ∘

In the cabin's kitchen, Winnie took the opportunity to look around. She tried to not be obvious. The place was a mess. There were two doors, but there was junk piled against the back door. She could see more trees through the windows; it was obvious that they weren't in the city anymore. She tried to find any little bit of information that could be important. She would try her dreaming experiment again later. She hoped that Gren would try to wander.

Number One stood next to her at the stove. He seemed oblivious to the fact that Winnie was on a fact-finding mission. He listened intently to everything that Winnie told him, he seemed interested in learning to become a better cook. "So what do we do next?"

Winnie continued to stir the pot on the stove. "And then you just add a little bit of seasoning."

"How do you know when you've added enough?"

Winnie laughed as she stirred. "You taste it, silly! Remember to add it slowly, though, because 'you can always add more, but you can't take away'. That's one of the first rules they taught us at school." Winnie picked up a different spoon and tasted some of the contents of the pot. "It's pretty good—but it's missing something. Remember, I'm first orbit, I have a long way to go."

She picked up a clean spoon and scooped out some more. "Here, you try it."

Number One took a step back. "Sure, Mollie, get me to take off my mask."

"I wasn't trying to, I promise," Winnie said, shaking her head. "I'll...I'll turn around until you say otherwise. I just wanted you to try it."

"I'm just teasing you, Mollie," One said, laughing. "But your turning around isn't a bad idea."

Winnie turned so her back was facing Number One. She took another look around the small room. The windows were so dirty! She couldn't see anything besides trees. A large branch hung down in front of the window.

"Okay," One said.

Winnie turned back around. "What did you think?"

One laughed again. "I think that you should do all the cooking around here."

"Holy splarsh!" The front door opened and closed.

Without thinking about the consequences, Winnie automatically turned and looked in the direction of the door. All she saw was a man's back. He had collar length dark hair, and was taller than Number One.

A micro or two later the door opened again. "What's the kid doing in here?" A mask severely distorted Two's voice. He had a bag in his hands.

One faced his partner. "Look, Two, you leave us here alone all rotation, I'm not going to keep her locked up by herself. And she has a name."

"I made you the evening meal," Winnie said, hoping to gain Two's favor.

"Put her back." Two's voice was stern.

Without another word, Winnie walked back to the other room. She already knew better than to cross Number Two.

"Sorry about him," One whispered to Winnie. He closed the door and locked it.

Winnie put her ear to the door and tried to listen. "And how come I have to be Number Two? This whole thing was my idea!" His voice was no longer distorted.

"Because I'm the one who spends the whole rotation here!" One started to laugh. "The *One*, get it?" He was obviously pleased with the pun.

"I get it." Two sounded disgusted.

"Bad rotation at work?"

Winnie could hear Number Two sigh through the door. "More of the same. Sometimes I have no idea why I even bother. But then something happens, like finding out about this kid. Anything new with her dreams?"

"No, she hasn't mentioned them," One replied. "And I'm not about to ask her. She has no idea why she's here. I figure letting her relax a little can't hurt."

"Premonition dreams can be brought on by stress," Two said. "Relaxing isn't what she needs. We need to make her think that she's in danger."

"Come, on, she's just a child!"

There was a pause. "We'll try it your way this one last time. But if there's no premonition tonight, tomorrow we'll use the tonic." Winnie heard a thud through the door. "Stole some from work. It shouldn't take too long to find the right combination."

Winnie lied back down on the bed. "How am I going to come up with a premonition?" she mumbled to herself. "Glen!"

"Gren, I need your help" she said.

Chapter Fourteen

Sham had what he thought was a brilliant idea. Titus wasn't so sure, but for some reason he decided to go along with him. They tried to follow Grey when they got out of work at the end of the rotation. They didn't make it very far. After trying to stay far behind and be as inconspicuous as possible, they found themselves at the same station where Gren and Lawson had met Winnie and Mollie. Since it was the final rotation of the work-third, the station was packed. It didn't take long for Grey to disappear into the crowd.

"That was useless," Titus remarked as they started the long walk home.

"Well I didn't hear you come up with a better idea!"

They argued the whole way home. Neither of them was really mad at the other, they were just frustrated with the situation. They were both surprised when they entered their dwelling. Everyone was there, but instead of the solemn mood that had been constant since Winnie's disappearance, they were all cheerful. Gren and Lawson were huddled together, looking over something intently, while Calli and Mollie worked in the kitchen. Tayo was sitting on the floor in the corner, trying to wander. She didn't seem to be having any luck finding Winnie, but even her mood seemed better.

"What happened here?" Titus whispered to his friend.

"I don't know," Sham replied, "but whatever it was, I'm glad that it did." He raised his voice. "Hey guys, we're back. Some of us still work for a living."

"Took you long enough," Lawson said without looking up. "Now go pack."

"Pack?" Sham repeated. "For what?"

"We're all going to Lake Collins for a couple of rotations," Lawson said. "I got a great deal on a cabin. I guess they figured it was better to give it to us at a discount than to let it stay empty for the rest of the lunar cycle."

"Lake Collins?" Titus asked.

Lawson nodded but didn't say anything else.

Sham took a few steps closer. "Listen Gren, Titus and I followed Grey after work today. We didn't get very far. I don't know if it means anything or not, but we lost him at the station. We couldn't find out where he was headed."

"The station? Sham, you're wonderful!" Gren jumped up, ran over to Sham, and gave him a hug. She went and sat back down.

"Hey, what about me? Lawson teased.

Gren shot a look Lawson's way. "You're wonderful too. But don't you see? That confirms it!"

"Confirms what?" Sham, still surprised by the embrace, knew that he was missing a large piece of information.

"Lawson and I went back to the Learning Center today," Gren explained. "Hutch says hello. He also told us that Grey and his brother own a cabin somewhere near Lake Collins. That's why he was going to the station, and that's where they're holding Winnie."

"Mollie had another dream," Lawson added. "It very well

could have been in that area."

"Grey and his brother?" Titus said. "Do you think that his brother is also somehow involved?"

Gren thought for a micro. "Hutch mentioned that Grey's brother works, although he didn't say where. The person with Grey seems to be spending all his time with Winnie, so he isn't working. It's got to be someone else."

"Gren!" Tayo screamed from where she sat in the corner. "I think I found her!"

* ○ ● ● ● ○ ○ *

"I'm okay, I promise," Winnie said. She sat on a bench in the park by herself, watching Mollie roll down a hill. "At least for now. I think we're in a cabin of some type. There are two of them. Number One has been really nice to me but I don't think that Number Two likes me very much. Gren, they think I'm Mollie."

"I know, honey," Gren's voice said. "Mollie has had a couple of dreams, so we think we know the area where they're holding you. We're coming. I need you to try to find out all the information that you can, anything that will help us to find the right cabin."

"I'll try." Winnie paused for a micro to listen to Mollie laugh. "Gren, they expect a premonition. If I don't give them one, Number Two is going to start experimenting with tonic."

"Give him something," Gren's voice instructed. "If he's done any research on Premonition Dreaming, he'll know that things can change. Have him trip in the kitchen, or bang his head on something. Anything that he can avoid by making a change. You've seen Mollie do it plenty of times, copy her body language when she has one of the dreams. And then just do what you're doing now."

"Okay, I'll try. Gren, there's one more thing."

"What?"

Winnie paused. "I think that Cassidy is somehow involved."

"Cassidy?" Gren's voice sounded surprised. "Why?"

"I've been thinking," Winnie explained, "and it's the only thing that makes sense. She's the one person, besides you and your friends, that even knows about Mollie's dreams. I just can't figure out why they grabbed me by mistake."

"It's not Cassidy," Gren's voice explained. "It's Grey, one of her apprentices. We think that he was listening at the door the rotation that we brought you and Mollie in to meet Cassidy. And the reason that they think you're Mollie is because of a picture in a book. You bear a striking resemblance to a girl that used to have premonition dreams. Grey must have seen the picture."

"Oh."

"Listen, honey, we probably should cut this conversation short. Grey is a Wanderer, he's probably checking from time to time to see if you're dreaming. We'll also keep coming back. We're taking turns, so it could be any of us. Keep trying to find information. Even the smallest little detail could help."

"Okay." Winnie stood up from the bench. "Gren, I love you."

"I love you too."

○ ○ ○●○ ○ ○

A unit later, they were all crowded into Calli's glidemobile. It hadn't been built for so many people, but no one seemed to mind. There was a new feeling of hope. Mollie was smiling broadly; it was the first time she had smiled since Winnie had disappeared.

Tayo was particularly excited. "I never thought that I could do it," she said to her partner. "Wandering distances just seemed impossible to me. That's advanced stuff! But I knew how important it was that we keep trying to find her, and since Gren and Lawson had said Lake Collins, I reached out in that direction. I couldn't really enter her dream, but I touched it, and somehow I knew it was Winnie. That was all it took. I was then able to steer Gren in the right direction. I knew she would be able to do it."

Calli grinned. "I'm proud of you, Tayo." An orbit earlier a similar conversation would have turned into an argument, but things had changed. "You really came through."

"So did you," Tayo said. "We've all had our parts in this. You were with Mollie when I found Winnie, which was important as well."

"It's too bad that it's not possible to pinpoint an exact location when wandering," Calli commented. "That would make finding her so much easier."

"Yeah, but it's not like wandering is an exact science…"

A little while later, seated in the back, Gren tried not to show her concerns. Mollie had just fallen asleep on her shoulder. Gren was happy that she had made contact with Winnie, was relieved that her sister was all right, but was worried at the same time. How long would they give Winnie to come up with a premonition? What would they do when dreams didn't start coming true? How long would Winnie be able to fake it? Gren had confidence in her little sister, she knew that Winnie was smart and had a lot of common sense, but there had to be a limit to Grey's patience. What would he do when he finally figured out that they had the wrong girl?

"We're not going to let it go that long," Lawson said quietly. "We'll have her back safely before Grey realizes anything."

Gren looked at Lawson. Wanderers couldn't read thoughts, and she hadn't been dreaming. "How did you know—?"

Lawson grinned. "Gren, this is me. We've been best friends since we were Winnie's age. I know you better than anyone does. I don't have to wander to know that you're worried. But Winnie will be fine. Grey may be annoying, but besides trying to fight with Sham from time to time I don't think he's violent. If he does figure it out, he'll just let her go. Winnie doesn't know anything and they've worn masks so she can't identify them. They have no reason to hurt her."

"Yeah, I guess you're right. It's just that—"

Without warning, Mollie sat up and opened her eyes. She didn't blink. Gren immediately recognized what was happening.

◦ ◦ ◖●◗ ◦ ◦ ◦

Winnie was at the door, listening.

"I don't care!" Number Two was screaming. "We need something, something real. Anybody could have tripped on a floorboard; my avoiding it because of her dream doesn't mean a thing!"

"She's just a kid." Number One's voice was filled with desperation. "You can't just start pumping her full of chemicals."

"Sleep tonic is perfectly safe," Two said. "It won't hurt her."

"You don't know that. How do you know she won't have some type of allergic reaction? We're out here in the middle of nowhere, how would we get help?"

"That's rare." There was a pause before Number Two spoke

again. "One more rotation. That's all the time I'm giving her to come up with something real, and then we're going to try it my way."

"Okay."

Winnie could hear the front door open. "I'm going for a walk; I'll be back in a unit or so."

"Okay," One replied. "I'll handle things from here."

The door closed. There was a creaking sound, followed by a loud crash.

"Holy splarsh!" Number Two screamed.

Winnie tried to see out the small window. All she could see were branches and leaves. Obviously, a large branch had broken off a tree. Winnie heard the door open again. She immediately returned to her listening spot.

"Come on in and sit down, I'll get you some ice," Number One was saying.

Taking a chance, Winnie knocked on the door. "One?" she called. "Is everything alright? I heard something outside."

"Don't worry, Mollie," One called through the door. "There's an old, dying tree out front, or rather there *was* an old dying tree out front. One of the branches gave way, with Number Two under it."

"Is he okay?" Winnie asked.

"Just a bump on the head, he'll be fine."

Mollie shook her head and looked around. It took a micro for her to realize where she was. "Did it happen again?"

Gren was writing furiously in Winnie's journal. "Yes, and Mollie, it was beautiful."

"It was?" Mollie seemed confused. "All I remember is a

crash and a bunch of leaves."

Gren finished her notes. "We now have something to give to Winnie. A dream that she can pass on that will come true. That should buy us some time." Gren closed her eyes and tried to reach out to her sister. She needed to pass the information on as soon as possible.

Chapter Fifteen

Winnie sat up on the bed. Even with her eyes closed, she knew that Number Two was in the room. She assumed that One was as well. She had been practicing ever since her contact with Gren. She had already pictured it in her mind dozens of times; she hoped that she could make it believable.

Allowing her mind to drift, Winnie formed the image of Number Two looking down on her. He wore the mask. He stared at her for a micro, shook his head, and then walked away. The light was dim in the room and as he neared the door, he tripped on a loose floorboard. She pictured it happening the same way two more times. She lay back down on the bed and pretended that she was asleep but not dreaming.

"What happened?" she heard Number One whisper.

"Shhh. I'll tell you in a micro."

Winnie felt Number Two looking down on her. She wondered if it was by the power of suggestion. He stood there for a micro or two. She heard him walk away. She knew that he was near the loose floorboard because of the squeak. His footsteps paused and then started again. She heard a second set of footsteps, followed by the closing of the door. As quietly as she could Winnie stood up and tiptoed to the door. She placed her ear against it.

"So *that* was wandering?" Number One asked. "With the amount that you people get paid I expected something more interesting than *that*."

"I was just observing," Two said. "A real wandering session requires interacting with the dream. And I don't get paid nearly enough. If my cheapskate boss would share some of the wealth, then we wouldn't even be here right now."

"Risking time in the Labor Camp," One mumbled.

"We're not going to get caught. We're isolated enough here."

"So what was the dream?"

Two sighed. "She dreamed that I tripped on a floorboard. All this time, research, and work, and she dreams that I trip on a floorboard."

"When does it happen?" One asked.

"It looked like it was supposed to happen right away. But I didn't trip, now did I?"

"But—" One sounded excited, "—but you stopped and walked around it before we came in here! I saw you do it! You told me yourself; sometimes the premonitions show things that can be changed. She had a premonition of you tripping, so you changed where you stepped. You changed the future. It *does* work!"

Two laughed. "I don't think we're going to get rich off of telling people to avoid loose floorboards. I'm tired, I'm going to bed."

Winnie returned to her own bed. The deception seemed to have worked, but for how long?

• • • ● ◐ • •

"Hey, Winnie, over here!" Mollie waved wildly in the distance. She stood in front of a giant, steaming pot. It was as tall as a building. There was a ladder against it. "I'm going in!" Mollie started to climb the ladder.

"Mollie, don't!" Winnie screamed. Her partner ignored her. Winnie ran as fast as she could until she reached the ladder. She could already feel the heat from the pot on her face. She put her foot on the ladder's bottom rung. "Mollie, wait for me!" She started to climb. The ladder was so hot that just touching it burned her hands, but she knew that she needed to save her friend.

"Get down from there, right now! Both of you."

"Gren," Winnie asked, "is that you?"

"Yes," Gren's voice said. "Now get down. I need to talk to you."

Winnie did as she was told. She sat down on the ground. Mollie and the steaming pot disappeared. "What happened? Where's Mollie?"

"Don't worry about that," Gren's voice instructed. "Mollie is safe, she's with me. Listen, I need you to concentrate. This is a real dream, and real dreams can be very hard to remember. Most importantly, how are you?"

"I'm okay," Winnie replied. "They haven't hurt me or anything. I did as you said, Gren. I made up a dream, something that easily could have happened. Two believed it, at least enough that he avoided the loose floorboard. But I think he's going to want something bigger."

"I might have it," Gren's voice told her. "Do you know anything about what is outside of the cabin where they're keeping you?"

"There's just a bunch of trees," Winnie replied.

"Mollie had another dream," Gren's voice said. "In it, you

heard the two men talking, then Two left. You heard a crash. Apparently a branch fell from a tree right in front of the cabin, and he was under it."

"Did he get hurt?" Winnie's question sounded slightly hopeful.

"Not badly."

"So what do I do with this information?"

"Find some way to give it to them," Gren's voice said. "Maybe tell One that this happened in a dream, since he seems more sympathetic to you."

"Okay, I'll try," Winnie replied. "Oh, Gren, before I forget, there are a couple of little things that I overheard. I don't know if they mean anything or not."

"Any information could be important."

"Number Two said that they're not going to get caught because we're isolated."

"Isolated," Gren's voice repeated. "That's a huge help. Anything else?"

"He called his boss a cheapskate." Winnie stretched and yawned. "It's been great talking to you, Gren, but I think I'm waking up now."

"Just remember, the branch from the tree crashes and Two gets hurt."

"Branch, crash, Two, ouch. Got it."

Sitting up, Winnie decided that she needed to act. She didn't want to fake another dream if possible, she had pulled it off but it had been difficult. She knew that she needed to do something immediately; she had no idea when Mollie's dream would take place but she knew that the time frame was usually just a few units. She decided to try the first thing that came to mind. She screamed. It was as loud and scary a scream as she could muster. Winnie then pulled her legs up, and then grabbed the covers from her bed. She rolled them into a ball and held them close, trying her hardest to look like she was terrified. She was about to scream again when Number One burst into the room.

The lights came on. "Mollie, what's wrong?" One adjusted his mask. He had obviously put it over his head in a hurry.

"Is...is Number Two okay?" Winnie made her voice crack as she asked.

"Of course he is. Why wouldn't he be?"

Winnie decided on the spot to make it seem like she believed that the dream was real. "There was a crash, out front. A branch from a tree fell, and he was hurt. You must have heard it!"

One shook his head. "There was no crash, Mollie, and Two is sound asleep."

Winnie stood up and took a few steps towards the door. "No, he's hurt! I know I shouldn't care, because he hasn't been very nice to me, but I'm more compassionate than that. We have to go look for him!"

"Mollie, if I show you that nothing happened will you let me go back to bed?" One asked. Winnie nodded. "Okay." Number One took Winnie's hand and they walked to the front door. He opened it.

Winnie took a couple of steps forward. The fresh air felt wonderful. She hadn't been outside since she was in the park with Mollie. She looked around as much as she dared. Isolated was definitely the word for it. There were no other cabins within view. They were slightly up, as if on the slope of a small hill. Winnie made mental notes about the crooked pathway that led up to the cabin and the unusual color of the glidemobile that was nearby. Most glidemobiles were silver or gold, with colored details. This one appeared in the starlight to be black, with white detailing. She looked up and around, counting the trees directly in front of the cabin. She saw the branch in question but decided not to point it out. Gren had said that Two wasn't badly hurt; she needed to let it happen. "Huh," Winnie said at last. "I guess you're right."

"Come on back in, Mollie," One said. "It's late, and I'm tired."

"I'm sorry." Winnie took one final deep breath of fresh air and reentered the cabin. Without being asked, she went right to her room.

One stayed by the door as Winnie fixed the covers and got back into bed. "Do you need anything?"

"No, thank you. Again, I'm sorry. I didn't mean to wake you up."

"Not a problem, Mollie. Get some sleep." One turned off the lights and closed the door.

Winnie grinned in the dark. She knew that she had made her point.

Chapter Sixteen

Everyone was up early the next rotation. Using the information that Winnie had passed on to Gren in her dream, they narrowed down where they would search. Claiming that they were isolated cut out several places that they might look, but Lake Collins was huge. Searching the less-populated areas could still take rotations, even if they broke up into groups.

"Tayo and I will start over here," Calli said, pointing at the map. "It's the furthest out. Why don't we drop you guys off here," she pointed again, "and here? Then we can all work our way towards the middle."

Sham was looking over Calli's shoulder. "Poke."

Calli took a deep breath and let it out slowly. "Since you're not a student anymore, that can work both ways." She jabbed her finger several times into Sham's arm. "Poke, poke, poke, poke, poke."

"Would you two cut it out?" Titus pleaded. "At least until we finalize what we're doing."

"Okay, sorry." Sham bent close and whispered into Calli's ear. "But later, it's war."

"Bring it on," she replied.

"Hey Sham," Gren called, trying to avert his attention, "I didn't know that Cassidy was tight with money."

"She's not," Sham replied. "In fact, I think she's pretty generous. Why do you say that?"

"Winnie told me that Grey had referred to her as being a 'cheapskate'."

"Cassidy told us that Grey is always looking for the quick and easy way out," Titus added. "Maybe that's what he was referring to."

"What's your payback percentage?" Calli asked.

Sham and Titus glanced at each other. It was a topic that they had always somehow managed to avoid around Gren and Lawson. "Ten percent," Sham said quietly, hoping that Calli would be the only one to hear.

Lawson heard. "Ten percent! You've got to be kidding me. Haas made us agree to twenty-five!"

"What's payback percentage?" Mollie asked.

"When you're apprenticing for a licensed Dream Wanderer, you get paid," Gren explained. "But since you're still learning and can't really do all that much, the boss is losing money for having you around. So the apprentice agrees to a 'payback percentage'. Once I'm licensed and practicing, twenty-five percent of what I earn the first five orbits will be paid directly back to Haas."

"Ten percent," Lawson mumbled, shaking his head.

"Just remember, Lawson, that you're apprenticing for one of the best in the business," Tayo said. "How long has it been since Haas even *had* apprentices? The name alone will make up for the difference."

"I hope so."

"I won't tell them that our payback time is three orbits, not five," Sham whispered to Calli.

"Back to our plan," Calli said. "Mollie, who do you want to search with?"

"Can I go with you and Tayo?"

"That's fine with me."

Gren looked slightly hurt. "Sure, Mollie, you can work with them."

"I'm sorry, Gren," Mollie said. "I'll go with you if you want me to. It's just I figured that you would be trying to contact Winnie a lot. If I'm with them, I'll have someone to talk to. Plus since they're going to be using the glidemobile, they'll have the most ground to cover. I thought that they could use an extra set of eyes."

Gren smiled. "It's fine. I'm glad you feel so comfortable with my friends."

"I think we should change up the teams a little bit," Sham said with as much authority as he could muster. "Make them all male/female. That way—"

"If the male runs into trouble there will be a female around to help?" Calli interrupted.

"Calli and I are a team," Tayo said, grabbing her partner's arm. "Remember how well we worked together last orbit? We're not splitting up."

"No one is splitting up," Gren said. "We keep our normal partners. Everyone ready?"

Each person nodded. They folded up the map and left.

∘ ∘ ● ● ∘ ∘

Their first stop was to drop off Sham and Titus. Sham stood next to the glidemobile. "Tell me again, what are we looking for? So I have it fresh in my mind."

"It's a cabin," Gren replied. "It's isolated. In the front there's a tree that has a branch that's about to fall or it's already broken off so it would probably be lying in front of the cabin. It's probably far away from the tourists since Grey thinks that they won't get caught. The windows are dirty, so it's probably not all that well taken care of. There are lots of trees. When Winnie has looked out the window she's seen lots of trees."

Sham glanced around. He already saw lots of trees. "Whatever you say."

"We'll do our best," Titus said quickly. He realized that it was a long shot that they would find anything, but he was happy to help look. "We'll be back out on the road in, what, three units?"

"We'll swing by and pick you up then," Calli told him. "We'll have something to eat and compare notes." Calli looked directly at Sham. "Don't forget where you've already looked. You wouldn't want to end up searching the same place twice." She grinned at him.

"I'll try to wander at the top of every unit," Gren said, "for just a hundred or so. If you find anything let your mind drift, but if there's no information don't do anything."

"Is Gren saying that there's no information in Sham's mind?" Calli whispered to Tayo, loud enough so that Sham could hear it.

Sham rolled his eyes. "See you in three units." He and Titus watched the glidemobile pull away. "You think maybe Cassidy is looking for a couple of new apprentices next orbit? I kind of like having Calli and Tayo around again."

Titus grinned. "Yeah, I can tell." *Especially Calli* he thought but decided against saying it aloud.

Gren and Lawson were next. The road where they started was a bit further out. It didn't look well-traveled. Before they started their search, Gren sat down and tried to reach out to Winnie. Her sister didn't seem to be dreaming. She stood up again, brushed off some dirt, and they started to walk. "Lawson, is this hopeless?"

Lawson put his arm around Gren's shoulder. "No, of course not. I mean, it's better than doing nothing. The System Workers are trying too, if we can't find her they will. But I think that we're going to find her. Call it a gut feeling."

"I hate this," Gren said. "I feel like I let Winnie down. Like I let my whole family down. If I hadn't been so excited about Mollie's dreams—" Gren started to cry.

Lawson pulled his best friend close to him and allowed her to cry on his shoulder. "This isn't your fault. Remember, Mollie came to you for help. You did exactly what you should have done—you tried to find out more information. How were we supposed to know that Grey was going to eavesdrop and decide that he could make money off of Mollie's dreams?"

Gren pulled away and wiped her face with her hands. "I still don't understand that. It's not like someone can pick and choose who they're going to dream about. What does he expect to do?"

"I doubt he's really thought things through," Lawson said. "We're talking about Grey here. He's not exactly the smartest person that we've ever known."

"He keeps talking about giving her tonics. If he read the same books that we did, he would know that there's no exact combination of the various tonics to produce premonitions. I hate the thought of him giving Winnie unknown amounts of tonics that have never been mixed together before. Lawson, she's just a child!"

"Sleep tonic is safe; you know that as well as I do. Besides, by giving her Mollie's dream last night you've bought her some time."

"But what if—"

"Shhh." Lawson held up a finger to Gren's lips. "You're not doing Winnie any good by making up scenarios. She's a smart girl. And it seems that Grey's partner is watching out for her as well. Grey may be an idiot, but he's not going to hurt a kid."

Gren nodded. "You're right. Thanks."

Lawson put his arm around Gren a second time. "Let's get moving, we've got a lot of ground to cover." Arm in arm they started down the road, not really knowing what they were looking for.

∘ ∘ ●◐● ∘ ∘

Calli and Tayo had held onto the map. They had been planning just to travel around the lake, looking for anything that seemed suspicious, but they had underestimated the amount of ground that they would have to cover. They rethought their plan and instead spent the morning marking off side roads and pathways that weren't included on the map. It seemed to them that if someone wanted to be somewhere isolated, the areas surrounding Lake Collins would easily supply the opportunity.

Before they knew it, it was time to pick everyone up. Three units had passed quickly. Sham and Titus were first. They were both dirty and tired, it was obvious that neither of them were used to hiking through the woods. The five of them then swung by and picked up Gren and Lawson.

Taking one look at his roommates, Lawson grinned. "It's no wonder that Hutch didn't believe me when I said that you love nature, Sham."

"I don't know," Sham replied. "Between the dirt and the bugs and tripping over things, I think this is paradise."

"At least it's not raining all the time, like when we were on Abacu," Tayo commented.

Mollie looked confused. "You were on Abacu? How is that possible?"

"Not the planet, Mollie," Tayo said quickly. "It's a long story."

"Anybody have any luck?" Titus said quickly, trying to change the subject. They weren't supposed to tell anyone about their trip to Abacu an orbit earlier. "We've at least ruled out a couple of places."

"We've been looking for more areas where they could be," Calli said. "There are so many back roads that it isn't even funny. This looks like a good place." She parked her glidemobile and they all got out. They had brought a picnic with them. They grabbed what they needed and headed towards the beach by the lake. Mollie helped Calli spread out the blanket and they all sat down.

"I wish that we had more to go on," Lawson said.

"Good idea. Let me see if I can find anything else out." Gren closed her eyes. She opened them again. "I can't try to wander if everyone is staring at me." She turned around so her back was to her friends.

"She's been trying to reach Winnie all morning," Lawson whispered.

"I still don't get how it works," Mollie said.

"Dream Wandering is a gift," Calli explained. "Something that people are either born with or they're not. It's one of the things that children are tested for during the placement process. Even if someone has the gift, it doesn't mean they'll become a Wanderer. It's a hard program to complete. If they don't complete it, the gift is removed."

"What we do is enter a dream," Lawson continued. "We can see what's happening. In a regular session, we guide someone through the rough spots. It helps to alleviate anxieties, stuff like that."

"So you can read people's minds?" Mollie asked.

Calli shook her head. "No, it's much more complicated than that. I can't tell what you're thinking, no one can do that. But you use a different part of your brain when you dream, and that's the part that we're able to enter."

"A black glidemobile." Gren's voice surprised everyone. She turned back around. "With white trim. The cabin is on a small slope, slightly high up. She called it a small hill. There are no other cabins within sight. The pathway leading up to the cabin is crooked. And there's a black glidemobile with white trim parked out front."

"How is she?" Mollie asked quickly.

"Winnie is worried about you, Mollie. Otherwise she's fine," Gren said, patting Mollie's hand. "And very, very smart. She was able to trick Number One into taking her outside last night. She got a really good look around."

"Grey doesn't own a glidemobile," Sham said.

"It's probably his partner's." Calli thought for a micro. "We didn't see anything like that when we were going around. I would have remembered a black glidemobile."

"They're fairly rare," Titus added. He knew more about glidemobiles than any of his friends.

"A black glidemobile?" Lawson scratched his head, thinking. "I know I've seen one recently."

Gren nodded. "I have too. But where?"

Chapter Seventeen

Winnie sat on her small bed, her eyes closed. She replayed the dream in her mind while it was still fresh. She saw herself on a park bench, watching Mollie roll down a hill. It had quickly become one of her favorite things to dream about. "It hasn't happened yet, Gren," she remembered saying aloud, even though she was alone.

"Doesn't it sometimes take a little bit of time?" Gren's voice asked.

"Yeah, I guess." Winnie paused. "I don't think that Number One realized that it was supposed to be a premonition. He just thought that it was a nightmare. Oh, Gren, I almost forgot! I tricked him into taking me outside! It was dark, but I got a pretty good look around."

"Great job. What did you find out?"

"We're on a small hill," Winnie started excitedly. "Slightly high up. I guess it's a hill, it's not really all that high."

"Did you see any other cabins?" Gren's voice asked.

"None," Winnie replied. "Isolated it the word! But there is a really crooked pathway leading up to the cabin. I don't know if that helps or not."

"That helps a great deal."

"And there was one more thing," Winnie continued. "There's a black glidemobile parked out front. Black! I've never seen one before. It had white trim. It's the weirdest looking thing."

"Black with white trim," Gren's voice mumbled. "That sounds familiar."

"Maybe it's Grey's?"

"I'll ask them," Gren's voice said. "How are you otherwise?"

"I'm good," Winnie assured her. "Number One has taken a bit of a liking to me, but Number Two is grumpy. I'm worried about Mollie. How is she?"

"Worried about you, but otherwise fine."

"Take care of her."

"We will," Gren's voice promised. "And you be careful. I'll be back in touch soon."

⋅ ⚬ ⚪●◍●⚪ ⚬ ⋅

After reliving the conversation with her sister several times, Winnie wasn't sure what to do. Number Two hadn't left for work like the previous rotations, she could hear his voice. Although she couldn't make out the words, it was obvious that he was upset about something. "I hope a tree branch *does* fall and hit you on the head," she mumbled to herself as she stood up. She tiptoed to the door and stuck her ear up against it.

"I don't care!" Number Two yelled. "We need something, something real. Anybody could have tripped on a floorboard; my avoiding it because of her dream doesn't mean a thing!"

"She's just a kid. You can't just start pumping her full of chemicals." Number One sounded desperate.

"Sleep tonic is perfectly safe. It won't hurt her." Two's voice was slightly calmer.

"You don't know that. How do you know she won't have some type of allergic reaction? We're out here in the middle of nowhere, how would we get help?"

"That's rare." Two paused. "One more rotation. That's all the time I'm giving her to come up with something real, and then we're going to try it my way."

"Okay," Number One agreed. It sounded like he had given up.

Winnie heard the front door open. "I'm going for a walk, I'll be back in a unit or so."

"Okay," One said again. "I'll handle things from here."

The door closed. There was a creaking sound, followed by a loud crash.

"Holy splarsh!" Number Two screamed.

Winnie hurried to the small window and tried to see outside. All she could see were branches and leaves. The branch that Gren had told her about had finally broken off. Winnie heard the door open again. She went back to the door to try to hear more.

"Come on in and sit down, I'll get you some ice," Number One said.

Winnie rolled her hand into a fist, held it towards the door, and then paused for a micro. She decided that it wouldn't hurt anything, so she knocked on the door. "One?" she called. "Is everything alright? I heard something outside."

"Don't worry, Mollie," One yelled back. "There's an old, dying tree out front, or rather there *was* an old dying tree out front. One of the branches gave way, with Number Two under it."

"Is he okay?" Winnie asked.

"Just a bump on the head, he'll be fine. Wait a micro—"

Winnie could hear some movement but wasn't sure what

was happening. She grinned; Mollie's dream had come finally true. She heard footsteps so she backed away from the door just before it opened.

One adjusted his mask as he entered the room. "Mollie, come on out here. I want you to tell Two what happened last night."

Winnie almost laughed when she saw Two. He was wearing the mask over his head, but held a bag of ice on top of it. He looked ridiculous. "Are you okay?" she asked sheepishly. "If it's a head injury, you should have someone look at it."

"Yeah, you'd like that, wouldn't you," Two said sarcastically. "I leave in my glidemobile, so you can work on One a little bit more."

Winnie shook her head. "I don't know what you're talking about."

"Sure you don't."

"Mollie," One said, hoping to change his partner's mood, "tell Two what happened last night."

Winnie decided to play stupid and stared blankly at One.

"The dream, Mollie. Tell Two about the dream."

"Oh, that." Winnie took her time before starting. She looked at Two and suppressed another laugh. "I had a dream last night. You were upset about something, I could hear you yelling. You left, and there was a crash. A branch gave way from a tree out front, and you were under it. Is that what happened? Is that how you hurt your head?"

Two suddenly looked interested. "Tell me about your dreams, Mollie. Do you often have dreams come true?"

"It happens sometimes. And sometimes after the dream, I'll tell the person and they can change the outcome, like you with the floorboard." Winnie was making things up as she went along, but it seemed to be working.

"Do you have any control over the dreams?" Two asked.

"Not really." Winnie decided to take a chance. Maybe it would make things easier on her. "They happen more often when I'm relaxed, not stressed out. Maybe that's why it happened. Cooking yesterday with One was almost enjoyable." She remembered that one of Cassidy's books had mentioned that stress could bring on the dreams; she hoped that her captors hadn't read the same book.

"There's no reason for you to stress out, Mollie," One added. "We're not going to hurt you."

"You've never even told me why you have me here."

Two adjusted the bag of ice. "Do you have any control over who the dreams are about?"

Winnie quickly shook her head. "No. But it's always about people that I know."

"Really?" Two put the ice bag on the table. "What about the glidemobile accident?"

"How did you know—?"

"Put her back," Two ordered One. "This little brat just lied to us."

One made a show of grabbing Winnie's arm. For the first time, she was scared. He pulled her back to the room that they had been keeping her in. "Don't worry, everything will be fine," he whispered to her before loudly slamming the door.

Winnie pressed her ear to the door for several micros, but no one said anything. She finally lay back down on the bed. "What have I done?" she mumbled to herself.

Chapter Eighteen

Gren and her friends spent the rest of the rotation searching for crooked paths to isolated cabins with black glidemobiles parked out front. They had no luck. Once it became too dark to search, they went back to their cabin to plan things out for the next morning. Sham and Calli carefully studied the map, each of them taking every opportunity that they could to try to poke the other by surprise. Tayo, Titus and Mollie were all close by, ignoring them.

Lawson sat on a large, comfortable sofa next to Gren. "This place is nice. Once we're official and in practice for ourselves, we should buy one of these cabins."

Gren managed a weak smile. "We? Aren't you being a bit presumptuous about our future?"

"Optimistic is more like it." Lawson put his arm around Gren and she relaxed against him. "We'll find her, Gren. We're getting closer."

The stress was obviously taking its toll on Gren. "I don't know how much more of this I can take. She's just a baby."

"She's not a baby," Lawson said, "and she's very capable. You've said it yourself, Winnie is very smart."

"She's been lucky so far. I hope she doesn't make a mistake." Gren yawned.

"Why don't you go try to get some sleep?" Lawson

suggested. "You're obviously exhausted."

"Let me try to reach Winnie one more time." The only movement Gren made was to close her eyes before she reached out to try to find her sister.

• ◦ ◑●◐ ◦ ◦

Winnie wasn't in the park. She sat in a chair in a hallway. She was alone. The sign on the nearby door read "Banner". Gren knew that Banner was the leader of the Culinary Institute. Winnie looked nervous, as if she thought that she was in trouble.

"Are you okay?" Gren's voice asked immediately.

"Gren, I've made a terrible mistake!"

"Tell me what happened. Did they hurt you?" Gren used every ounce of strength that she had to keep her voice calm, as if it was a professional wandering session.

"They didn't hurt me," Winnie replied. "But I messed up so badly, and I don't know how to fix it."

"Tell me what happened," Gren's voice repeated.

"Mollie's dream came true," Winnie started. "The branch fell and bonked Two on the head real good. One came and wanted me to tell Two about the dream. Everything was fine. He was really interested in the dreams, no big surprise. He even seemed to believe me when I said that stress makes the dreams happen less often. One was really nice about that, saying that they wouldn't stress me out. But then Two asked me if I have any control over the dreams, and that's where I got in trouble."

"What did you tell him?"

"I said that I have no control, but that the dreams are always about people that I know." Winnie paused. "Gren, he somehow knew about the glidemobile accident that Mollie saw in her dream. He knew that I was lying about knowing the people."

"What happened next?" Gren's voice remained steady, not showing the fear that she was feeling.

"He told One to put me back in my room. One whispered to me that everything will be okay. I listened at the door for a little while, but neither of them said anything. Two brought me the evening meal tonight and didn't say a word to me as he did it."

"Don't worry," Gren's voice said. "One sounds like he's watching out for you. And we're continuing to search. I don't know how much longer I can keep contact right now, though. I really need to get some sleep."

"Gren?" Winnie called. "There's one more thing. Two referred to it as 'his' glidemobile, and One didn't correct him. I don't know if that means anything or not."

"That's a big help." There was a yawn in Gren's voice. "I'll talk to you again soon. I love you."

"I love you too."

⋄ ◦ ◦ ◉ ◦ ◦ ⋄

"What happened?" Lawson knew by the look on Gren's face that something was wrong.

"Grey caught Winnie in a lie," Gren explained. "She's really worried about it. At least his partner is still watching out for her. But I'm scared that we're running out of time."

"Anything else from Winnie?" Lawson asked.

"Yeah. Sham..." Gren called out, "I thought you said that Grey doesn't own a glidemobile."

"He doesn't," Sham said.

"I've heard him mention wanting one to Cassidy," Titus added. "He was asking her to up his pay a bit, but she wouldn't budge."

"That could explain the cheapskate comment," Calli remarked.

"Winnie said that Two referred to it as being *his* glidemobile," Gren said. "Strange."

"Probably just a figure of speech," Tayo said.

"Probably." Gren sat up and stretched. "I'm going to bed. We have another long rotation ahead of us, so I would suggest that all of you do the same."

                    ◦ ◦ ● ◗ ◦ ◦

It was a dreamless night. Maybe it was because of exhaustion, but everyone slept so soundly that no one remembered his or her dreams. Gren had been secretly hoping that Mollie would have had another premonition that she could pass on to Winnie, but it didn't happen.

Their search was much the same as the previous rotation. Gren made contact with Winnie a couple of times, but there was nothing new. The only bit of useful information that she had been able to find out was that Number Two had a nasty bump on the top of his head from where the tree branch had hit him. Winnie reported that he complained of it hurting each time the mask would touch the top of his head.

That evening Gren shared the information with her friends during the evening meal. "Winnie said she can always tell if Number Two is about to come in because she'll hear him grunt."

"It warms my heart to know that Grey is in pain." Sham tried to poke Calli, but she grabbed his finger.

"Is Winnie still okay otherwise?" Mollie asked.

"Yeah," Gren promised. "She said it's been a pretty quiet rotation. She's hardly seen Number One at all, and Two only for meals. There hasn't been a whole lot of conversation between the two of them either, so she hasn't had much of a chance to eavesdrop. She does know that Two has to go back to work tomorrow."

"Speaking of which," Calli said, "I think I need to get these two back home." She let go of Sham's finger and motioned with her head towards Titus.

"You're leaving?" Mollie asked.

"We'll be back in a few units," Calli promised.

"I don't know how I'm going to work tomorrow," Sham said. "Looking at Grey's ugly face and knowing what he's done—"

"Sham, please," Gren said. "We can't let Grey know that we're onto him. And when you're at work, take a good look around for a black glidemobile. He's got be to hiding it somewhere."

Chapter Nineteen

Titus was nervous about heading to work. Not only did he wish that he could still be up at Lake Collins to help with the search, but he also was dreading Sham's reaction when they first saw Grey.

As they walked, Sham wouldn't stop talking. "Just wait until I get my hands on him. When I think about what he's done to poor Winnie! Gren is putting on such a brave front, but I know that it's tearing her apart. And Calli was supposed to be here on vacation…"

Titus stifled a laugh. "I was wondering how long it would take."

"What?"

"For you to turn the conversation around to Calli."

"I haven't turned the conversation around to Calli. I've hardly even thought about her."

"Right." Titus grinned. "Tayo is here on vacation as well, but you didn't even mention her."

Sham grew defensive. "Grey has me so upset that I didn't even have a chance."

"Right. And that's why you're spending all your time poking Calli?"

Sham laughed. "She's fun to poke. It drives her crazy."

"You're such a good friend, Sham."

Cassidy had arranged for different wandering sessions for Titus and Sham. She seemed as if her mind was elsewhere. "Everything okay?" Titus asked.

"It's been a long morning," Cassidy replied. "My husband was gone for a couple of rotations, and he had a minor accident while he was away. He wasn't badly hurt, but he's almost unbearable when he has a headache! Now come, the client is in here..."

Titus found it odd that Cassidy didn't ask if there was any news on Winnie but decided not to mention anything.

After his session was over, Titus went to look for Sham. Titus knew that Sham was going to go looking for Grey, promise to Gren or no promise. He just hoped that Sham was able to control his temper. It didn't take long to find them, but Titus was too late. Sham and Grey were already in a back room, antagonizing each other.

"At least I made it through the whole program without having to change partners every other rotation," Sham yelled. "What did you do, look at your partners and scare them away?"

"The only reason you kept the same partner for so long was so that you could cheat off of his tests," Grey shot back. "Everyone knows that there was no way you were smart enough to actually pass."

"I never cheated. And Titus and I stayed together because we work well together. We're *friends*. I know that's a concept that's totally foreign to you."

"Sham..." Titus warned.

Sham ignored the warning. "The reason you're so weird, Grey, is that no one cares about you. No one has *ever* cared about you. Not even your mother—"

"Sham!" Titus yelled, but it was too late.

"Why you..." Grey balled his hand up into a fist.

Titus rolled his eyes and stepped between Sham and Grey. Once again, he took the full brunt of the punch. He fell to the ground. "Would you two cut it out? You hate each other, so just ignore each other."

Grey shook his hand from the force of the hit. "Titus, stop getting in the way. One of these rotations I'm really going to hurt you, and he's not worth it."

Sham snuck up behind Grey. He flattened his hand and brought it down as hard as possible on the top of Grey's head.

Grey looked at Sham as if he was insane. "What do you think you're doing?"

"Didn't that hurt?" Sham's surprise was obvious.

"No, but if you want me to hurt you..."

Sham grabbed Titus' arm and pulled him to his feet. "Come on, we've got to talk. Later, Grey."

∘ ∘ ◦●◦ ∘ ∘

A hundred later, they were hidden in a storage closet. Titus was rubbing his eye, which he could feel swelling. "You want to tell me what that was all about?"

"Sorry about that, Titus," Sham said. "Grey is right, you really need to stop getting in the way. I can take it, you know."

"You promised Gren you wouldn't antagonize him."

"No," Sham corrected, "I promised Gren that I wouldn't let him know that we're on to him. Big difference. If I *didn't* antagonize him, Grey would be suspicious. But it doesn't matter, because Grey isn't Number Two."

"How do you know that?"

"Winnie told Gren that Two is grunting every time he puts the mask on," Sham explained. "The top of his head really hurts—from the tree accident. You saw what I did; I bonked Grey as hard as I could. He obviously doesn't have a sore head. Deranged, maybe. Ugly, definitely. But sore, no."

Titus sighed. "I guess if my taking one helped us find out some information that could help Gren, it was worth it."

"But now we have to start all over again."

Titus shook his head. "Maybe not. Don't you think it's a little bit weird that Cassidy hasn't even asked us about Winnie?"

"Yeah. So?"

"She told me that her husband was gone for a couple of rotations," Titus said. "That he had an accident, and now has a bad headache. Maybe she knows that Winnie is okay, because it's Cassidy's husband that grabbed her. Remember that she told us once that they own a cabin up at Lake Collins. It makes sense."

Sham shook his head. "Cassidy knows that the wrong kid was grabbed."

Titus paused, thinking. "Maybe she's expecting us to do exactly what we're doing. Have Gren pass along Mollie's dreams. Or maybe her husband made the initial mistake but Cassidy knew we'd do something to try to find Winnie, so now they're waiting for an opportunity to grab Mollie as well. Sham, we've got to warn Gren!"

∘ ∘ ● ● ∘ ∘

Less than a hundred later Sham and Titus were talking to Olosa, Cassidy's receptionist. Titus had his hand over half his face.

"It was totally a freak accident," Sham lied. "Titus tripped, and down he went. He claims he's okay, but it looks terrible. So I want to take him to the Medical Center and have him checked out."

"Let me see it," Olosa said, moving towards Titus. She tried to pull his hand away. "I started training as a Medical Practitioner but was moved to—Holy splarsh, you're right. You need to have someone look at that, Titus."

"I'm okay," Titus replied, pulling away.

Olosa stared at Titus. "Are you sure it was an accident, and not Grey? When I saw him a few micros ago he was shaking his hand, like it hurt."

"Good," Sham mumbled.

"Sham is the one who can't get along with Grey, not me," Titus said quickly. "Come on, Sham, let's go."

"I'll let Cassidy know that you had an emergency and left," Olosa called behind them.

It started to rain as soon as they stepped out of the building. "Great," Titus said, pulling his coat up over his head.

"Titus," Sham started, "maybe Olosa is right. Maybe you should have someone take a look at that eye."

"On Olosa's recommendation?" Titus laughed. "It's not that bad, even though it hurts like crazy. Just so you know...I don't forgive you."

"I didn't ask you to."

The two friends were soaked to the skin by the time they made it to the station. "Maybe we should try to contact Gren," Titus suggested. "You know, like Lawson does. We could warn her without having to head all the way out to Lake Collins."

"I've watched Lawson dozens of times, I'll do it." Sham sat down on a bench and closed his eyes. Between being soaking wet and sitting with his eyes closed he must have looked quite peculiar. Everyone who walked by stared. After a hundred, Sham opened his eyes. "Might as well buy the tickets, Titus, I couldn't reach her. I don't know how Lawson does it."

"*Me* buy the tickets? I thought you were paying for them. After instigating Grey like you did, you owe me!"

Sham stood up and reached into his pocket. "I didn't ask you to get in the way. And you're never going to let me live it down are you?"

Titus grinned. "Nope."

Chapter Twenty

Looking out of the small window in her room, Winnie saw that it was still dark. Through her door she could hear One and Two moving, but there were no voices. Ever since her mistake, if she heard them talk it was always in the distance. She was sure that Two had figured out that she had been eavesdropping and was making sure that it wouldn't happen again. "I'm going to be so stinking late!" was the only thing that she heard Two say before the door slammed shut. She expected One to come in and talk to her but it didn't happen.

A couple of units later the door to her room finally opened. Winnie had fallen back to sleep. "Mollie, time to wake up!" One's voice said cheerfully. "Come on out here. You can eat with me; you're probably getting sick of having crumbs in your bed."

Winnie sat up and stretched. She wondered how One planned to share a meal with her with his mask on. He had made a big deal out of it when she had asked him to just taste the food that they had prepared together. It seemed like orbits ago. She meandered out of her room.

"Good morning," One said. There was a single place set at the table.

The upbeat tone of his voice worried Winnie. "I thought we were going to eat together."

"No, I already ate," One said. His voice was almost melodic.

"I just wanted you out here with me. Mollie, I need to talk to you."

Winnie sat down and took a bite of her food. It wasn't bland like Number One's previous attempts.

"Not bad, huh? See, Mollie, in the short time that you've been here, I've learned a lot."

"What did you need to talk about?" Winnie asked.

"Go ahead and finish your meal first. It can wait." Number One walked over and stared out the window while Winnie ate. "Looks like it's going to rain."

Winnie ate quickly. She had a bad feeling about the conversation that they were about to have. "I'm done. Thank you."

One took away the plate and placed it in the sink. He sat down next to Winnie. "Mollie, I can understand why you lied to us, and I don't blame you. You don't want to be here, you're supposed to be on vacation. What we've done by bringing you here, well, it isn't right, and I'm sorry I got involved to begin with."

"Why did you do it?" Winnie asked.

"Two, well, he had big plans," One explained. "He made it sound so easy. I guess I didn't think of you as being a real person when he was explaining his idea. And now, I'm in so deep…"

"I won't tell anyone that it was you," Winnie promised. "Just let me go. Tell Two that I escaped."

One shook his head. "I can't do that. He'd…anyway, that's not what I wanted to talk about. After what happened with the tree, Two wants to try to speed things up. He knows that your dreams can come true, and he wants to make that happen. So when he gets back tonight he's going to give you something to drink. It's called 'Sleep Tonic', and it won't hurt you, I promise. It will just make you dream."

"I can't control what I dream," Winnie said. She felt nauseous and wished that she hadn't eaten anything.

"Two has done some research. It's thought that premonition dreams can be brought on using a combination of various tonics. He just needs to find the right combination and give you a suggestion. Since you already have the dreams, he's just going to guide them in the direction that he wants."

Winnie put her head down and started to cry. She didn't know what to do.

One patted her on the head. "There, there, Mollie, it's not that bad."

Winnie looked up and wiped her eyes. "My name's not Mollie."

"What?"

"Mollie is my roommate, my partner at school," Winnie said. "She's the one who has been having the dreams. We came here on the break because my sister asked us to. She's a Dream Wandering apprentice, and I thought that maybe she could help. Mollie really wants the dreams to stop."

One sat back, believing every word. "Then who are you?"

"My name is Winnie."

"What about your dream? You knew that the branch was going to break, with Two underneath it."

"That was Mollie's dream," Winnie said. "Gren, my sister, is really good. She can wander distances. She wandered Mollie's dream and watched it happen, then wandered my dream and told me about it. I woke up and screamed, and then I told you what Gren had told me."

"So you've been in contact with your sister?"

Winnie nodded. "She doesn't know where we are, though, just the place to look for my dreams. Dream Wandering is very complicated."

"So I've heard."

"So One, you've got to stop Two from giving me the tonic," Winnie pleaded. "It's not going to give me premonition dreams, and Grey scares me."

"Grey?" One asked. "Why did you call him Grey?"

Winnie looked confused. "Isn't that Number Two's real name?"

One shook his head. "No. Why would you think that?"

"I...I was trying to figure out who knew about Mollie's dreams," Winnie said. "There's an apprentice named Grey who works with a couple of Gren's friends. He's about the same height as Two. I assumed that he had listened at the door when we were explaining the dreams to his boss."

"You'd know all about eavesdropping, wouldn't you, Moll—Winnie."

"Sorry about that."

One sighed. "We can't let Two know what you've told me. He wouldn't believe you anyway, since he's already caught you lying. Tell you what...fake sick tonight, a bad stomachache. Stick your finger down your throat if you need to. He'll think you won't be able to keep the tonic down and won't want to waste it. That will buy us some time."

"Then what?"

One patted Winnie on the hand. "I'll take care of you. I won't let anyone hurt you, Winnie. I promise."

Chapter Twenty-One

The sky was dark. Although the rain hadn't yet started, it was just a matter of time. Instead of breaking up and searching in two groups, everyone stayed in the glidemobile. Although no one voiced it, they all feared that they were running out of time.

They drove slowly up a long, crooked path that led to a secluded cabin on a small hill. For the first time in rotations, they felt a little bit of hope. There was no glidemobile parked out front. "Grey would have left for work, so the glidemobile wouldn't be there," Lawson reasoned.

Calli parked her glidemobile close enough so that they could see the cabin, but behind a tree to give them some cover. They stayed inside the vehicle and looked around. The cabin wasn't in great condition. Even from the outside it was obvious that it could use a good cleaning. There was a fresh-cut stump near the front door. "Maybe they cut the tree down after the branch fell," Tayo said.

"So what's the plan?" Mollie asked.

"Mollie, you're staying here," Gren said immediately. "Calli will stay with you, won't you Calli?"

Calli nodded, the disappointment obvious on her face.

"But I—"

Gren took Mollie's hands. "Mollie, they already have Winnie.

I'm not going to risk losing you as well. You're the one that they really wanted. You can't get near them. Do you understand?"

"Fine."

"So what *is* the plan?" Tayo asked.

Gren thought for a micro. "I guess we just knock on the door. If this is the right place and they answer, it would just be Number One, and we could reason with him. If they don't answer, I'll ask Winnie next time I wander if she heard someone knocking. There's a rhythm that I used to do when she was younger—she'll understand."

"Are you sure that we can't come too?" Mollie asked.

"Yes." Gren leaned forward to Calli as she was about to get out of the glidemobile. "Be ready to go for help," she whispered.

Gren, Lawson and Tayo walked towards the front door. Lawson walked slightly ahead of the two girls, as if he were there to protect them from an unseen foe. When they reached the door he went to knock on it, but Gren stopped him. "My special rhythm, remember?" Gren knocked on the door twice fast, three times more slowly, and then twice fast again. She counted to twenty and then started the same pattern again.

The door flew open. "What do you want?" A man stood before them. He was short, balding, and heavy.

"Oh..." Gren stammered, "I'm looking..."

"Honey, who is it?" a female voice asked from inside.

The man turned for a micro. "Just a bunch of kids." He turned his attention back to Gren. "You were saying?"

"We were hiking," Lawson said quickly. "We kind of got lost. The cabin that we're staying at looks a lot like this one. Do you know of any more in the area?"

"Yeah," the man said. "There are two groups of them that I

know of. There are probably a dozen or so right around here, and then they made an identical retreat on the other side of the lake. But if you were hiking then your cabin wouldn't be over there. Just head back out the way you came and you'll reach the main road. The paths to the cabins all branch off from it."

"Honey, who is it?" the female voice repeated.

"Just a bunch of kids," he called back again. "They got lost hiking, can't find their cabin."

"I hope they find it soon, it looks like it's going to rain," the woman commented.

"She's right," the man said to the group in front of him. "Looks like we're in for some nasty weather."

"Thank you, Sir," Lawson said, shaking the man's hand. "You've been very helpful."

They heard the door close as they walked back towards the glidemobile. "That was pointless," Tayo remarked.

"Not at all," Lawson said. He seemed excited. "He just told us where we should look! He said that there are two groups of cabins like this. It shouldn't take too long to check the dozen cabins on this side. Then there's another group on the other side of the lake. That's it! I was so excited when I tricked him into telling me that."

Gren grinned. "You've been having a lot of great moments lately, my friend."

· ⚬ ⚬◯● ◯⚬ ⚬ ·

Winnie was sitting on a cot, resting her chin on her hands. The dream wasn't any form of escape, which worried Gren. It told her that Winnie was starting to worry. "Hey there. You need someone to talk to?"

"Gren!" Winnie jumped up off the cot and looked around,

then remembered that her sister wasn't actually there. She sat back down. "Gren, there's so much that I need to tell you. Everything is such a mess."

"What happened?"

"I told One the truth, that I'm not Mollie. I had to! He told me that Two was going to give me tonic tonight, and I knew that meant he would start expecting me to have dreams. I really don't like Two, Gren. I think that even One is scared of him."

Gren tried hard to stay in her best wandering mode. She needed to keep her voice calm. It was difficult to do, especially hearing the fear in Winnie's voice. "I'll admit that I don't know Grey well, but he never struck me as being dangerous."

"It's not Grey," Winnie said.

"How do you know?"

"I mentioned the name by accident," Winnie explained. "I didn't mean to, but it was right after I told One the truth. He had no idea what I was talking about."

"It's not Grey," Gren's voice mumbled. "What else did you tell him?"

"I said that you and I have been in contact. I didn't say how much, but I had to explain my knowing about Mollie's dream. I didn't tell him that you're up here trying to find me."

"How did he react to all of this?"

Winnie smiled for the first time. "He was really nice. I'm going to fake being sick tonight so Two won't give me the tonic. One promised that he's going to help me. I'm not really sure how, but I trust him...at least as much as you can trust a kidnapper."

"Use your instincts," Gren's voice instructed. "They've always been strong. Is there anything else you can remember, anything that might help us find the cabin?"

Winnie thought for a micro. "No, I've told you everything." She turned, as if she thought she heard something. "I think that One is about to come in here."

"Okay. I'll talk to you soon. We're getting close. You'll be back with us before you know it."

· · ● ◉ ● · ·

The whole group had returned to the cabin. Lawson and Tayo studied the map, although they had it memorized. Calli talked with Mollie, trying to distract her. Gren was wandering. She soon opened her eyes and stared ahead, not wanting to accept the information. She slowly shook her head.

"Is Winnie okay?" Mollie asked, worried.

"Oh, I'm sorry. She's fine. I just can't comprehend what she just told me." Gren didn't say anything else.

"What?" Lawson asked after several micros.

"It's not Grey," Gren told her friends. "Someone else took her."

"How do you know?" Calli asked.

"She mentioned Grey's name to Number One by mistake. Winnie said he didn't know what she was talking about. One seems like he's going to help Winnie. She said she trusts him." Gren stood up. "Lawson, could you help me? I stuck something on the top shelf of the closet and I don't think I can reach it—"

"Sure." Lawson followed Gren into one of the bedrooms. "Lame excuse, Gren. What's wrong?"

Gren's face showed her fear. "Winnie told One the truth. He knows that she's not Mollie. Lawson, we're running out of time."

There was a loud knock in the background. "Gren, Lawson,

someone is here," Calli called from the other room.

Lawson rushed out first and went to the door. The rest of the group stood behind him. "Who is it?" he called.

"Lawson, just open the stinking door!" Sham yelled. "We've got something important to tell you."

Sham and Titus were a mess, totally drenched and covered with mud. Calli couldn't help but laugh as they entered the cabin. "I'd like to see you walk all the way here from the local station," Sham said to her.

"I'm sorry," Calli said, laughter still in her voice.

Gren was more concerned with Titus. "What happened to you eye?"

"Sham's plan happened," Titus mumbled.

"Long story; short version," Sham said. "We got into a fight with Grey at work. Titus took the punch, while I bonked Grey on the top of the head. It didn't hurt him." Everyone stared at Sham as if he was insane. "Don't you see what this means? Grey isn't the kidnapper!"

"We know," Tayo said calmly.

"You know?" Sham was upset, but wasn't sure why.

"Winnie found out," Gren explained. "I just talked to her." She looked at the whole group. "I think we should still search around Lake Collins. It makes sense. We know she's at a cabin, and we know that Two goes back and forth from work every rotation."

"And we know that Two is Cassidy's husband," Titus added calmly.

Chapter Twenty-Two

They had come up with a plan. Winnie knew exactly what to do. When Number Two brought her the evening meal she was already laying on her cot, curled up. "I'm not feeling very well," she complained.

Two didn't reply.

"I don't know if I can—"

"Just eat it." Two put the tray down and left.

Winnie ate what he had left her, glad that she had given Number One a few cooking tips. It still wasn't great, but it was better than before. She finished, counted to ten, and then moaned loudly. She went into the small necessary room, took a deep breath, and stuck her finger down her throat. It was disgusting, but she was willing to do it if it meant that she wouldn't have to take the tonic. She coughed several times, and then did it again. "One?" she called feebly.

One and Two both came running. "Mollie, are you okay?" One asked.

"I feel really sick. I told *him*," Winnie glanced at Two, "before, but he didn't seem to care. He made me eat it anyway."

One put his hand on Winnie's forehead. "You don't have a fever. Clean yourself up, and then get a good night's sleep. I bet you'll feel better in the morning."

"Okay," Winnie replied.

Two left the room first, mumbling to himself as he went. "Can't give her tonic if she can't keep it down. I don't believe this. Another night wasted…"

One glanced back at Winnie and nodded slightly. Winnie winked in reply.

○ ○ ● ◉ ● ○ ○

The next morning Winnie woke up to a banging sound. She went to her door and tried it; if Number Two hadn't yet left it would be locked. It opened. Number One had a couple of bags on the table. He was furiously trying to find things to fill them. There was stuff spread out everywhere. "Is there anything I can do to help?"

One opened a cabinet, looked inside, and then slammed it shut. "Good morning, Winnie. Yeah, if you could grab us something to eat that would be great. Something that we can eat on the go. Then get yourself ready, because we're leaving."

"Where are we going?" Winnie asked.

"I'm taking you home."

○ ○ ● ◉ ○ ○

A unit later, they were ready. One had packed two backpacks. The first one was bulging full and looked quite heavy; the second contained a couple of thermal blankets, two rain coverings, and a few small items.

One was studying the map on the table. "I'm going to get you to the station," he explained. "But we can't take any of the roads, because Two will find us. We need to kind of make our own trail, something that isn't visible from the road. We're going to have to hide in the woods for a couple of rotations, hike around the long way. Eventually we'll use the river as our guide. We're here," he pointed on the map, "and the station is all the way over here, on the other side of Lake Collins. Do you mind hiking?"

"No," Winnie replied. She was excited; soon she would be back with Gren and Mollie. "I haven't really done a whole lot of it, but it will be an adventure, right?"

"Anything is better than what we've already put you through. Winnie, I'm so sorry."

Winnie smiled. "I'm glad you were involved. The way I'm thinking of it, if it weren't you, Two still would have had someone help him, someone not nearly as nice. When I get back with my sister, I'm going to tell the System Workers that you helped me. I'll do my best to make sure that you don't get in trouble for it."

"Thanks, Winnie, but I deserve any punishment that I get." One took one last peek around to make sure they didn't forget anything. "We'd better get moving. There's no telling what Two will do when he finds that we're gone. We need to put as much distance between us and this cabin as possible."

"You're scared of him, aren't you."

"Yeah, I guess so, at least scared of what he might do. But he wasn't always like this. Oh, one last thing." One reached up and took off the mask, revealing his face for the first time. He placed the mask on the table. "By the way, my name is Bryce."

• ◦ ⬤ ◦ ◦ •

They walked for several units. It wasn't an easy hike. Bryce was sure that Number Two would follow and wanted to make it as difficult for him as possible. They stopped often to rest and to drink water. Winnie was already worried about Bryce, his pack was heavy and there were times that he seemed to be struggling with it. She mentioned her concerns when they sat down to have something to eat. "Are you sure you don't want me to carry something else? My pack is a lot lighter than yours."

Bryce laughed. "I help grab you from the park, drag you away from you sister and your friend, hold you against your will, and you want to help me? You're quite a girl, Winnie."

"That's not how I see it." Winnie took a sip of water. "You've watched out for me ever since Two came up with his plan. If it weren't for you, I would still be stuck in that room. Two would have forced me to drink the tonic, realized that I'm not Mollie, and would be extremely upset now. Somehow I don't get the feeling that he would have then just taken me back to Gren's."

Bryce shook his head. "No."

Winnie looked up. The trees were thick where they were, but the sky was still visible. "At least it's not raining. It's not a bad rotation for a hike."

"We're going to be sore tomorrow."

"Probably."

Bryce paused. "Listen, Winnie, I've been giving it a lot of thought. When we get back, I'm going to turn myself in. I'm not going to shirk my responsibility here. I'm also going to cooperate, tell them who Two is and how to find him. I'll tell them the whole plan."

"I'll do whatever I can to help," Winnie promised. "I'll let them know how you've helped me. How did you get messed up in this, anyway?"

Bryce sighed. "I don't know. Two and I have known each other for most of our lives. We grew up in the same area. I didn't make it into any of the specialized programs, but he was accepted to the Learning Center to become a Dream Wanderer. I was so jealous! We used to come up here on school breaks, that cabin has been owned by his family for generations. But then there was an accident. Two's parents died. It was ruled that it wasn't his fault, but Two changed. I tried to be there for him, to be a good friend, but it wasn't easy. He threw himself into his work, from what he says he became really good at it, but his boss didn't seem to notice. Still doesn't. The accident was orbits ago but has affected everything he's done since. He got involved in a few things that you're too young to know about. And he started running up debts. His glidemobile, for example. Do you have any idea how expensive a black glidemobile is?"

Winnie shook her head.

"But anyway, a few rotations back he came to me. I had just lost my job because the business closed, and I was having a hard time finding a new one. Two told me that he had a plan that was going to take care of all our problems. A way to make easy money. He never even filled me in on the plan—I had no idea what he was doing. He picked me up that rotation; he was really upset about something. We followed you and your friends. He was the one who physically grabbed you, and by the time I realized what was going on, I was already in too deep. I didn't know how to make things right, so I played along. I'm so sorry, Winnie."

"You're scared of him." It was the second time that Winnie had made that observation.

"Yeah, I guess so. That's why I haven't told you his name. You need to know as little information about him as possible, in case he finds us. I've told you too much already." Bryce decided to change the subject. "So…have you tried getting in touch with your sister since we left?"

"No. To do that I need to let my mind wander into a dreamlike state, and then she has to try to find me. The timing has to be right, and it's kind of hard to let your mind drift like that while hiking."

"If you want to try now, go ahead."

Winnie pulled her legs up under her and put down her head. She closed her eyes. She tried to just let go of everything but couldn't do it. "I don't think it's going to happen. Sometimes it's hard to turn off my thoughts. Besides, Gren would have to be trying to wander. As I said, the timing has to be right."

"Then let's get moving," Bryce said. "I want to cover as much ground as we can before it gets dark." They both stood up and started forward. "I've been hearing about wandering almost my entire life and I still don't understand how it works."

Winnie grinned. "That makes two of us."

◦ ◦ ● ⬤ ● ◦ ◦

Slipping the mask over his head, Two entered the cabin. He had made the mistake once of assuming that the child would be locked in her room, not in the kitchen with Bryce. "That fool," he muttered to himself as he closed the door behind him.

Things were strangely quiet. "One?" he called out. Something was wrong. Things were a bigger mess than usual, cabinets and a closet door had been left open, and there was junk just left all over the place. "Mollie?" He was growing more upset by the micro. The door to the room where they had been keeping the child in was wide open. He stuck his head in, no one was there. "One, where are you!"

He walked over to the table to look at the things that were on it. Something caught his eye. He picked up the mask that his partner-in-crime had used since the kidnapping and held it in his hand. Suddenly, he understood. He knew that they were gone. "Bryce, I'm going to find you. And when I do, you're going to be sorry that you betrayed me."

Chapter Twenty-Three

The group was huddled together. Winnie and Mollie were holding onto each other tightly. Someone else was there, walking towards them. He was laughing. In his hand was a strange device with flashing lights.

"Noooo!"

○ ○●◉●○ ○

"Can you remember anything else?" Lawson asked Gren.

Gren shook her head. She was sitting up on her bed, cradling Mollie in her arms. The child was crying. "The dream was just a flash this time. I saw you, me, Mollie and Winnie, Calli and Tayo, and some guy that I didn't recognize. Calli was a mess, her uniform was ripped, and there was a cut on her face."

"No Sham or Titus?" Lawson asked.

"No," Gren replied.

"That's some important information," Lawson said. "Whatever was going on probably happens when they're at work."

"Which is most of the time," Gren reminded him. "I'm going to have to buy Calli a new fuel cell because of all the traveling that she's been doing." She paused. "The man that was in the dream. Not the guy with us, the other one. I didn't see his face, but he was somehow familiar."

"His laugh, maybe?"

"I don't know," Gren said. "The 'me' in the dream was reacting strangely. I can't explain it."

"Was it Cassidy's husband?" Lawson asked.

"I don't know." Gren bit her lip, thinking. "I've never met him, but Cassidy has a picture of him on her desk. I don't know if that's it or not."

"Maybe," Lawson started, "you reacted because you had seen it already. The 'you' in the dream would have already seen the dream, so living it would be a really weird sensation. Right?"

"I guess."

"At least we know to watch out," Lawson said, trying to lighten the mood a bit. "The dreams aren't a reflection of the future as much as a future that *could* be if things don't change. And we also know that we're going to find Winnie."

Mollie looked up and wiped her eyes. "Gren, after we find Winnie, are you going to be able to make the dreams stop? I don't want them anymore."

Gren held Mollie closer. "I'll do my best, Mollie. There's got to be a way."

· · ○ ○ ● ○ ○ · ·

Calli and Tayo returned from taking Sham and Titus home, and then the group that remained set out again. Since the rain had stopped, they decided to split up. Calli dropped Gren and Lawson off so that they could continue to search around the same area where they had been looking the previous rotation, while the rest went to the other side of the lake.

"Do you think there's any truth to Sham and Titus' theory about Cassidy's husband?" Gren asked her best friend.

"I don't know," Lawson replied. "The way that they

explained it made sense at the time, but just because someone had a headache doesn't make him a kidnapper. Their theory would make a lot more sense if they had grabbed the right kid." Lawson stopped, noticing the look on Gren's face. "I'm sorry, that didn't come out right. I'm just trying to put all the pieces together. The fact that they also own a cabin up here makes me think that maybe it *is* Cassidy's husband."

Gren stopped. "What if we're searching in the wrong place? What if it's not Lake Collins at all?"

"We have to believe that she's here," Lawson said. "Although wandering can't give someone a precise location it can give you a sense of direction, and Winnie's dreams have been this way. Also, the cabin in her dreams looks a lot like these. She's got to be somewhere around here."

"What if we're wrong?"

Lawson put a hand on Gren's shoulder. "We know from Mollie's dream last night that we find her. We just need to change the circumstances that take place after we do."

"I think we should take a quick break." Gren sat down and closed her eyes. Lawson knew that she was trying to wander. Gren opened her eyes again. "Nothing. It's the fifth time today that I've tried. It's never taken me this long before."

"Maybe she..." Lawson started, but wasn't sure how to finish.

"Maybe Two is around—keeping a close watch on her to make sure she's okay. She did say she was going to fake being sick. Or maybe he found out she wasn't really sick and has decided to make her pay. Or maybe he forced her to take the tonic and he realized that..."

"Stop right there," Lawson said. "I searched myself last

night. Tonic leaves traces, you know that as well as I do, and there wasn't anything. No one anywhere around here took any tonic. It's probably just a timing thing, that's why you can't find her. You know as well as I do how hard it can be to coordinate dreams, and that's when we *plan* it. Just reaching out from time to time, it's a miracle that you and Winnie have been able to communicate as much as you have."

"We need a miracle right about now."

The micro the words left Gren's lips, Calli's glidemobile pulled up behind them. "Gren, Lawson," Calli called excitedly, "I think we found it!"

○ ○ ◔ ● ◔ ○ ○

It took over a unit to make it to the other side of the lake. Tayo and Mollie had stayed behind so that they wouldn't lose the path. They stayed well hidden, in case anyone else came by. Calli stopped to pick them up.

"Gren," Mollie said excitedly, "it was here!"

"What?"

"The black glidemobile! It went up the path almost a unit ago, then a few hundreds it later left again."

"He was in a big hurry," Tayo added.

"Did you get a look at the driver?" Lawson asked.

Tayo shook her head. "It all happened too fast, plus I wanted to make sure that Mollie was well hidden. But I did see enough to know that he was alone."

"So now would be a good time to take a look around," Gren commented. She was excited; her sister could be close by. "If it's just Winnie and Number One, we should be okay. She did tell me that he promised to help her."

The crooked path seemed a lot longer than it actually was.

"What's the plan?" Mollie asked as they grew closer.

"Same as before," Lawson said quickly. "Calli and Mollie, you stay back. Gren, Tayo and I will see if they'll let us in."

"But—"

"It's especially important that you stay back," Gren told Mollie. "One knows that they don't have you."

"But you said he promised to help Winnie," Mollie argued.

"Yes, but he's still a kidnapper," Gren said. "There's no telling what he might do if the person who is having the actual dreams shows up."

"Okay," Mollie said, defeated.

There was no place close to hide a glidemobile, so Calli had to go partway back down the path. Gren, Lawson and Tayo got out and approached the cabin. "There it is!" Gren whispered, excitement in her voice. "The branch! It doesn't look like they moved it too far after it fell."

Lawson pointed. "That must be the dead tree."

"I'll do my special knock again," Gren said. "That way Winnie will know that we're here."

"You won't have to," Tayo said. "The front door is wide open."

They approached cautiously. Even with the door open Gren knocked twice fast, three times more slowly, and then twice fast again. "Hello?" she called. "Is anyone here? We were hiking, and…"

Lawson walked into the cabin and looked around. "There's no one here," he called. "At least not now."

Gren and Tayo entered. Gren immediately checked each room, just in case her sister was hiding somewhere. "Winnie?" she kept calling.

"Lawson, look at this." Tayo picked up the mask from the table and handed it to him. "Looks like someone has shown Winnie his face."

"Must have been Number One. He promised to help her, that has to be what's happening now. He's trying to get her home."

Gren joined her friends. "She's not here," she said sadly.

"My guess is that One is trying to get her away." Lawson held up the mask. "Look at what Tayo found."

Gren sighed. "At least now I know why I haven't been able to reach Winnie all rotation. I've been wandering in the wrong place."

"Where do you think they're going?" Tayo asked.

"Probably headed to the main Lake Collins Station," Lawson said. "Winnie only mentioned one glidemobile, so they'd have to walk to get there."

Tayo shook her head. "Wouldn't we have passed them on the road?"

"Not if they didn't take it," Gren replied. "If they're trying to stay away from Two they would avoid the road. They're probably hiking through the woods."

Tayo nodded in agreement. "So how are we going to find them? Start hiking too?"

"We have no idea how much time or distance they have on us," Lawson pointed out. "We'd never catch up."

"So we start at the station," Gren said. "Meet them in the middle."

"We could just wait at the station," Tayo suggested.

"No," Gren said quickly. "Too much could go wrong. Two isn't going to just let them go, he'll probably also be waiting at the station for them. There's strength in numbers, we need to find them."

"Come on," Lawson said, heading towards the door. "Let's go fill Calli and Mollie in on what's going on. Be sure to leave things exactly as you found them."

Taking one last glance around, they walked out of the cabin—leaving the front door open.

Chapter Twenty-Four

They hiked along the perimeter of the lake without getting too close. Once every unit they would take a break and Winnie would allow her mind to drift, hoping that Gren would be there. "Either she isn't trying at the same time or she can't find me," Winnie told Bryce. "She once tried to explain about direction to me, but I didn't really pay much attention."

Bryce smiled. "Yeah, it gets kind of boring listening to someone brag about wandering all the time."

"Gren never meant to brag, but she did anyway. I guess you talk about what you know. She's really gifted."

"I'd much rather hear about your gift," Bryce said. "The Culinary Institute, that's really impressive. It's a hard school to get into, even for someone recommended for Culinary Arts. You must have scored near the top of the test."

Winnie looked down modestly. "I guess."

Bryce stood up, helped Winnie to her feet, and then picked up his pack. "Let's get going. So, Winnie, tell me. What are your plans for the future?"

"The future is still way out there, I'm just a White." Winnie looked down at her dirty uniform and laughed. "Although I think that right now the color is debatable."

Bryce started to walk again. "I'm serious. You must have a

dream. If this were your last orbit, what would you be hoping to do?"

"I sometimes think," Winnie started slowly, "that I'd like to open my own restaurant. Mollie and me. Something different. Maybe Abacuan cuisine."

Bryce looked at Winnie as if she was insane. "Abacuan?"

Winnie giggled. "Not the planet, silly. Abacu is also the name of a region on the other side of Terra. Although I've never tasted their food, so I don't know if it would be good for a restaurant or not."

"Probably a good idea to find out first whether or not you like it," Bryce said. "There could be a reason that there aren't a whole lot of Abacuan restaurants around."

"You could be my assistant!" Winnie said. She sounded excited at the idea. "We've already proven that we work well together."

Bryce shook his head. "If I'm out of the Labor Camp by then."

"Please, Bryce," Winnie pleaded, "stop talking like that. I don't want you to go to the Labor Camp. I'll do whatever I have to, tell them whatever you want me to—"

"And they'll say that I brainwashed you. No, Winnie, what I did was wrong, and I'm going to accept whatever happens."

Winnie looked stubbornly at Bryce. "I'm still going to try to help."

Bryce grinned. "Winnie, just knowing that you forgive me is all the help that I need. I just want to get you back home safely."

• ◦ ◐ ● ◦ •

They continued until it was almost dark. Bryce started a campfire, and Winnie cooked the evening meal over it. "Be careful," Bryce kept saying, worried that Winnie was going to burn herself.

"You sound just like my parents," Winnie teased.

After they ate, they sat back and stared at the stars while the fire died down. "Do you think that there's life on other planets?" Bryce asked.

"Yeah, definitely," Winnie said. "There are so many out there, how could ours be the only one that supports life?"

Bryce sighed. "I think about that sometimes. How maybe there are people somewhere, just like us, but because the circumstances were slightly different *everything* is different. Everything we do affects us, we just don't always know how."

"What do you mean?"

"Take, for example, your placement exam," Bryce said. "What if you had gone to bed a unit later the night before? You might not have been as well rested, so you might not have had such a high score, so you might have entered a different culinary program, and then you never would have met Mollie. You wouldn't be here now."

"I get it," Winnie said.

"Even little things can make a difference. If Haas hadn't taken a micro to straighten a picture he wouldn't have fallen, and his practice would have gone on as normal."

Winnie thought for a micro. "How do you know about Haas falling?"

"Two is a Wanderer," Bryce said quickly. "I bet that every Wanderer in the city knows about Haas' accident. He is, supposedly, the best in the business. Listen, Winnie, we'd better get some sleep." He pulled the two bedrolls out of her pack. "We're probably going to be very sore tomorrow." He had said it several times throughout the rotation.

"Being sore and on my way back to Gren is better than being locked in that room," Winnie said. "And before you say it, please don't apologize again."

° ° ●●● ° °

Winnie was on her back, staring up at the stars. For the first time in rotations, everything seemed peaceful.

"Nice night, isn't it?"

Winnie sat up and looked around. "Lawson? Is that you? Where's Gren? Is she okay?"

"Relax, Gren is fine," Lawson's voice promised. "She just needed to get some sleep herself. She's really tired—she's been trying to find you all rotation. So I decided to try to wander."

"We left the cabin this morning," Winnie said.

"I kind of figured that out when we found it and you weren't there."

"You were at the cabin? So if we had just stayed, I'd be home by now?"

"Never mind that. It's good that you got away from Number Two. We're pretty sure that he was there after you left but before we showed up, so who knows what would have happened if we had all been there." Lawson's voice was calm but in control. "Where are you now? And what's your plan?"

"Bryce and I are headed to the station," Winnie said. "We're going around the perimeter of the lake. There's a road, not the main one but a secondary path that we're keeping track of that Bryce said should lead us there. We're not actually on that road but we're using it as a guide. We're also headed towards the river."

"We'll look it up on the map," Lawson's voice said. "We'll

start the other way, from the station, and try to meet you in the middle."

"I'll tell Bryce and we'll keep an eye out for you."

"That's the third time you've mentioned the name 'Bryce,'" Lawson's voice observed.

"Bryce is Number One," Winnie explained. "He's helping me get home. He's going to tell the System Workers everything when we get back. He's a really nice guy."

"Nice guy or not, you still be careful."

Winnie laughed. "Lawson, you can't tell me what to do, you're not my brother. Or my brother-in-law. So...just between you, me, and this dream, are you in love with my sister or not? What are your intentions towards her? I'm not really sure what that means, but I've heard my dad wonder about your intentions to mom late at night when they thought I was sleeping."

"I'd better go—big rotation tomorrow."

Winnie laughed again. "That's what I thought."

"We'll see you soon," Lawson's voice promised. "You'll be home before you know it."

Winnie put her head back down. "Lawson, thank you."

Alone in the cabin, the man known as Two sat in the dark. "They're traveling around the perimeter, towards the river, and Bryce is going to turn me in," he said aloud. "Yes, Lawson, thank you."

Chapter Twenty-Five

"Sham, Titus, in my office," Cassidy said. "I'll be there in a hundred. We need to talk."

"Great," Sham said to his former partner, closing the door behind them. "What did we do now?"

"We'll find out soon enough," Titus remarked. Sham took a seat but something caught Titus' eye. He walked over to the disorganized bookcase in the back of the office. He picked up a picture. "Sham, look at this."

Sham took it and stared for several micros. "I guess that tells us all that we need to know."

"So what do we do?" Titus asked.

"Come right out and ask Cassidy about the picture. Her reaction should tell us if she's involved or not."

The door opened and Titus quickly took a seat. Sham placed the picture behind him.

"Good morning, boys," Cassidy said, staring at some papers in her hand. She put them on the desk and sat down. "Titus, how's the eye?"

"It's feeling better."

"Well it doesn't look it." Cassidy stared at them over the top of the huge pile on her desk. "Boys, the two of you been distracted lately. I'm very close to giving you both your first warning."

Titus involuntarily gasped. Three warnings meant that they would never be able to obtain their licenses.

Cassidy continued. "Now I know that you've both been worried about your friend and the missing girl, but that's still no excuse. I'm sure that by now the System Workers are very close to finding out the truth. But it's not just that. Titus, would you like to tell me how you *really* hurt your eye? Keep in mind that Grey has a nasty bruise on his hand."

"I fell," Titus lied.

"Protecting Grey," Cassidy said. "I hope that's the start of the three of you attempting to get along. Now Sham, do you want to tell me why you have such a guilty look on your face? And show me what you're hiding behind your back? Keep in mind that I grew up with five brothers, I know that look."

"Oh, it's nothing, really." Sham pulled out the picture and handed it to her. "Titus and I were just admiring this when you came in. Black glidemobiles are rare. That's your husband, right?"

Cassidy smiled. "That was the rotation he bought that stinking thing. I swear he loved it more than he loves me! Cried like a baby when he crashed it."

Sham and Titus exchanged glances. "But he got it fixed, right?" Sham asked.

"No," Cassidy said. "It was totaled. It took him a couple of lunar cycles, but he finally grew to love the replacement. His nice, silver glidemobile that doesn't stick out when he's going by. Of course, that's now being repaired. Crashed that one a couple of rotations ago. I think I might have mentioned that he had been in an accident." She sighed. "Some people shouldn't be allowed to operate glidemobiles."

Sham and Titus exchanged glances again. Sham cleared his throat. "So your husband wasn't involved in Winnie's kidnapping?"

Cassidy laughed. "Is that why you two have been acting so strangely around me? What on Terra would make you think that?"

"I...we...I don't know..." Sham stammered, unable to come up with a good reply.

"We know that the person who took Winnie is a Dream Wanderer," Titus explained. "Someone who knows about Mollie's dreams. And someone who owns a black glidemobile. And we're also pretty sure that they took her to a cabin near Lake Collins. You had mentioned that you have cabin up there..."

"My husband isn't a Wanderer, he's an Engineer," Cassidy told them. "But it looks like you've found out a lot of information. A Dream Wanderer with a black glidemobile and a cabin near Lake Collins. Sorry, I don't think I know anyone like that."

"I do."

Sham and Titus both jumped as Grey flung the door open.

"Please, Grey, take a seat," Cassidy said. She pointed at the chair farthest away from Sham and Titus. "If you tell us what you know, you won't get a warning for eavesdropping."

Grey sat down, glanced at Sham and Titus. "I swear, I didn't know what was going on until now. I mean, I knew that something was up with you two, you've been acting even more annoying than usual, but I didn't realize that there had been a kidnapping. If I had known what he had done, I would have told someone. Endangering a child..."

Cassidy put up her hand. "Grey, you're getting ahead of

yourself. Tell me what you know."

"Back a few rotations ago, when Gren was here with those two girls, I overheard what was going on."

"You mean you were listening at the door," Sham corrected.

"Sham!" Cassidy said. "Don't. Let him speak."

"Fine," Grey continued, "I was listening at the door. I heard the whole story, about how the kid was having the premonition dreams, including the one where the people died in the glidemobile accident. The whole concept was fascinating, so when I saw my brother later that rotation I asked him about it. At first he brushed it off, but when I told him that it involved Gren, he suddenly became very interested. He can't stand Gren or Lawson."

Titus looked confused. "Gren and Lawson don't know your brother. If they did, they would have mentioned something to us."

"My brother works for Haas," Grey said. "He wanted me to apprentice there, but Haas wouldn't hear of it. 'I don't take apprentices' was what Haas said over and over again. So I applied here. Then all of a sudden, there were Gren and Lawson. He has no real reason to hate them, he just does. He hates Haas too, always complaining about how cheap he is, won't share his wealth, won't give him the opportunities that he thinks he deserves…"

"Haas can be a bit harsh," Titus said. "We hear that from Lawson all the time."

"Does your brother own a black glidemobile?" Cassidy asked.

Grey nodded. "Yeah. And we have a cabin up by Lake Collins."

"Has he been acting strange lately?" Cassidy asked.

"I haven't seen him in several rotations," Grey replied. "Ever since I asked him about the premonition dreams. And before you ask, yeah, I think that it's possible that he would do something like this. When our parents died, he changed. At first I thought that the change was my fault, he was upset about being saddled with the responsibility of caring for a minor, but even after I graduated and moved out on my own he was still bitter. He also doesn't always think things through. I'm sure he immediately came up with a plan to make money off the dreams, without even understanding how they work. I hope that she's had some of the dreams, to keep him interested."

"He grabbed the wrong kid," Sham commented.

"No." Grey stood up, a panicked look on his face. "We've got to get to the cabin. There's no telling what he'll—"

"Take my glidemobile," Cassidy said. "It's out back. I'd go myself, but I have clients."

"I'm not going with *him*," Sham objected.

"Sham, will you get over yourself for once?" Grey yelled. "Not only do I know where the cabin is, but he's my brother. I might be able to get him to listen to me."

Titus grabbed Sham by the arm. "Grey is right. Let's go."

"'Grey is right,'" Sham mumbled. "I never thought I'd hear you say those words."

● ● ●●●● ● ●

A few hundreds later, they were on their way. Titus was at the controls, and Grey sat in the front. Sham was in the back, mumbling to himself. Cassidy's glidemobile was quite a bit smaller than Calli's. Titus headed towards the main road.

"No, there's a shortcut," Grey informed him. "Take this next right." Titus did as told. There was an awkward silence. "So," Grey said at last, "when are you guys going to tell me what's been going on?"

"I thought you knew," Sham replied immediately. "Listening at the door all the time."

"Well if you would just—"

"Gren..." Titus said loudly, trying to stop the argument before it started, "...had her sister Winnie and her partner come to spend the break with her. Winnie and Mollie are both Whites at the Culinary Institute."

"Good school," Grey said.

Titus nodded. "Calli and Tayo from the Learning Center came too, to help take care of the girls during the rotation while Gren is at work. You might remember them, they're Blues this orbit."

"Calli and Tayo," Grey repeated. "Sounds vaguely familiar. Aren't they always arguing?"

"Not anymore," Sham mumbled.

"They've overcome their differences," Titus said. "But anyway, Mollie has been having dreams that have been coming true. She wants them to stop. Winnie thought that maybe Gren could somehow help. We all did some research, then a few rotations ago someone grabbed Winnie at the park."

"Are you sure we should be telling him all this?" Sham asked. "After all, it's his brother that took her!"

Titus ignored Sham. "Gren can wander distances and has been able to wander some of Winnie's dreams, so we found out a few things. Winnie realized right away that they thought she was Mollie, so she played along."

"She listened at the door," Sham said. "You two would

probably get along, you have a lot in common."

Titus continued to ignore Sham. "We know that there are two men, and that one of them is a lot nicer to Winnie than the other."

"That's probably Bryce," Grey said. "He's an old friend of my brother's. I can picture him playing along, but in the long run, he's harmless."

"What about your brother?" Titus asked. "Is he harmless?"

Grey paused. "Just let me be the one to talk to him. So how did you figure out that they're at Lake Collins?"

"Hutch told Gren and Lawson that you and your brother have a cabin up there," Titus replied.

"Wait a micro. You already knew that it was my brother?"

"No," Titus said, slightly embarrassed. "We thought that it was you."

"Oh."

○ ○ ◉ ○ ○ ○

A couple of units later they were at the cabin. "He's not here," Grey said.

"We can see that," Sham added. "It's not like a black glidemobile is easy to hide."

"Let me go first," Grey said. "I've known Bryce my whole life, I'm sure I can talk him into letting Winnie go."

Sham and Titus stayed back while Grey ran up to the cabin. They watched as he opened the door and went inside. "It's hard to believe that Winnie is in there, and that we're finally going to get her back," Sham commented.

"I know what you mean," Titus agreed. "I can't wait to see the look on Gren's face."

"Hey guys!" Grey was standing by the front door, trying to

get their attention. "They're not here. But they were. Come see what I found."

Sham and Titus ran to the cabin.

"Look," Grey said, holding a mask in his hand. "There's another one on the table. Looks like they were trying to keep her from seeing their faces."

"We already knew they were using masks," Sham said.

"So why are the masks here?" Titus wondered.

"And this..." Grey opened a cabinet. Inside were several bottles of different types of sleep tonic. "I bet he was planning on trying to mix them, make the dreams happen more frequently. I read about that."

Sham was growing angry. "You wouldn't have known about any of this if you hadn't been eavesdropping! Why did you have to go running to your brother?"

"I didn't go running to my brother!" Grey yelled back. "I just asked him if he had ever heard of premonition dreams, and he wanted to know why. So I told him what I had overheard."

"So you're admitting that this whole thing is your fault!"

"It's not my fault! I didn't know that he was going to come up with some crazy plan to make money off of the kid!"

"But if you hadn't been eavesdropping..."

"Stop it!" Titus yelled, but it was too late. He took a step forward as Sham threw a punch at Grey. Titus took the full brunt of it, falling to the floor. "Stop," he said, placing his hands over the bruise that he could already feel forming on his jaw. "I am so tired of this. We need to all get along, at least now, for Winnie's sake."

Grey held out a hand to Titus and helped him up. "I'm willing to try if he is."

Titus looked at Sham. "Well?"

"Fine." Sham grinned. "I got you good, didn't I? Sorry about that."

Titus shook his head. "One of these rotations, I'm going to be the one doing the hitting, not the other way around."

"Maybe in your dreams, my friend."

Chapter Twenty-Six

"Tell me the dream again. Maybe you left something out."

Lawson knew that he hadn't left anything out, but he didn't mind another retelling. For the first time in rotations, Gren seemed to have a little bit of hope. "They're hiking through the woods. They're going around the perimeter of the lake, and they're keeping track of a secondary road."

"That's got to be this one," Calli said. She approached them, map in hand. "See, it's pretty deep into the woods, nowhere near where most of the tourists would go. It's a long way around, but that makes sense. Number Two would probably assume that they would take the most direct route, so Number One is taking a longer one."

"His name is Bryce," Lawson said.

"What else did Winnie say?" Gren asked.

"That was about it. She said that Bryce is a nice guy. She seems to trust him. I guess that's a good thing."

"Here's what I'm thinking," Calli said. She pointed to the map. "If the cabin is here and they walked all rotation, they should be about here. So we should start looking about here, and then we'll meet them somewhere in the middle."

"We need to be careful," Gren said. "Winnie has good instincts, but we can't forget that Bryce did agree to a kidnapping."

"She said that he's going to tell the System Workers everything," Lawson said.

"Saying it and doing it are two different things." Tayo was standing off to the side. "When he thinks enough about it, he might change his mind. No one wants to go to the Labor Camps."

"But he still is helping Winnie," Lawson added. "My guess is that he'll take off as soon as we have her. Too bad, because someone needs to pay for what they've put the kid through."

"I don't care about that," Gren said. "I just want my sister to be safe."

"Here's what I'm thinking," Calli said again, drawing attention back to the map. "We don't want to overshoot them, so I'll drop you and Lawson off about here. I doubt that they've made it that far. Tayo, Mollie, and I will go along the path towards the cabin and back. Winnie knows what my glidemobile looks like; if she sees it maybe she'll flag me down."

"Your glidemobile looks like every other glidemobile out there," Mollie said. "She won't notice it, especially if they're hiding."

"It still won't hurt to try," Calli said. "At least it's not black, and she knows we're coming."

"So what are we waiting for?" Gren asked. "Let's get going."

· ◦ ◦ ● ◦ ◦ ·

Lawson was unusually quiet as he and Gren walked. Calli had dropped them off half a unit earlier and he had yet to say a word. At first Gren thought that he was listening, trying to find a sign of Winnie and Bryce, but soon she realized that it was more than that. "What's wrong?"

Lawson continued to avoid looking directly at Gren.

"Nothing."

"Lawson, this is me. We've been best friends since we were Winnie's age. I can tell when something is wrong."

"Nothing is wrong."

"Okay," Gren conceded, "nothing is wrong. But something is on your mind. What are you thinking about?"

"Nothing."

"Is it something to do with Winnie? Something from the dream?" Gren stopped, and grabbed Lawson's arm. "That's it, isn't it? Something happened in her dream, and you don't want me to know about it."

"Relax," Lawson said, a slight grin on his face. Gren really did know him well! "Yes, it's something from the dream, but not what you're thinking. Winnie made a comment, that's all."

"A comment about what?"

Lawson still avoided Gren's gaze. "Are they that obvious?"

"I still don't know what you're talking about."

"My feelings for you," Lawson said with a sigh. "Winnie asked me about them. And my intentions."

"Your intentions?" Gren laughed. "Winnie is just sticking her nose in where she shouldn't. You know very well that she considers you family—she's known you her entire life. There is nothing that she would like better than for it to become official. But you are family already, so don't let her bother you." She threw Lawson a playful glance. "And yes, they *are* that obvious. When we're finally licensed, we'll figure it all out."

* ∘ ∘●○ ∘ ∘

Calli continued to lead her glidemobile along the road that they thought Winnie and Bryce were using as a guide. They started near the cabin and tried to backtrack. They didn't return all the way to the cabin, they had estimated how far a man and a young girl could walk in a rotation and started there. Mollie had her face right up against the window the entire time. "Look, I think I see something!"

Calli pulled to the side and they all got out. Mollie ran into the woods. Tayo tried hard to keep up. "Mollie, wait! Slow down!" she called. "We don't want to lose you too!"

Mollie paid little attention. "Calli, Tayo, there's someone up ahead!" She ran even faster.

Tayo pushed herself harder and caught up with Mollie. "Where? I don't see anything."

"There." Mollie pointed.

"What's going on?" Calli asked, finally catching up to them.

"Mollie thinks she sees something." Tayo was still trying to catch her breath.

"I did see something. Over…there it is again."

There was a moving flash of something brown. Mollie ran towards it again.

"Mollie, wait!" Tayo called again.

The three of them ran through the undergrowth in the direction of the brown blur. As they neared it, Calli tripped on a loose vine and fell hard. Her blue uniform ripped and she received a nasty slash on her face. The vine had wrapped itself around her ankle and she struggled to free herself. "I'm okay," she immediately said to her partner. "Keep an eye on Mollie."

Mollie didn't even know that Calli had fallen. She followed the blur to a small clearing, where Tayo caught up with her. "That's not exactly who we're looking for," Mollie said sadly.

"No," Tayo said, putting an arm around the child's shoulder, "but they're beautiful. I sometimes see rolthers up at the Learning Center, but never this close." They stared at the rolthers for a micro as the animals stopped to drink. It appeared to be a mother and her offspring.

"Do you think the baby is a boy or a girl?" Mollie asked.

"A girl," Tayo replied. "Look at her coloring. I've heard that the females have light spots but the males' spots are dark when they're young."

The mother rolther picked up her head and stared at her admirers. "Can we pet her?"

Tayo smiled. "Looks like she might let us, but I don't think it's a good idea. Even though rolthers are gentle creatures they *are* wild animals, and mothers can be very protective of their young. I think we should just admire them from a distance."

"I wonder if Winnie has seen any rolthers."

"Probably. There are a lot of them around here. Come on, Mollie, we'd better get going."

Taking one last look, Tayo and Mollie started back. Calli was still on the ground, fighting with the vine. She didn't seem to be making much progress.

Mollie gasped. "Calli, your face!"

"I'm okay," Calli said, frustration filling her voice. "I'm just having a little bit of a problem with—"

"Here," Tayo said, reaching for the vine. She quickly untangled it.

"Thanks," Calli said. She rested for a moment. "I take it that was a false lead?"

"It was a couple of rolthers." Tayo held her hand out to her partner and helped Calli to her feet.

"A mother and a baby," Mollie said. "They were beautiful."

"And I missed it? Come on, we'd better get back to the

glidemobile." Calli kept a step or two back from Tayo and Mollie, trying not to limp as she walked.

· · · ● ○ · ·

Gren and Lawson walked quietly for a long time. Gren couldn't help but wonder if they were even in the right place. The entire situation was frustrating her. "Why do we even have to look for Winnie?" she asked at last. "Why aren't the System Workers doing their jobs?"

"It's not exactly like we've told them everything," Lawson said. "We never told them about Mollie's dreams, or how you've been wandering Winnie and have found out quite a bit of information. We didn't mention our suspicions about Grey or now Cassidy's husband, and if we had, they would have laughed at us. They base their work on facts and let's face it, wandering has little to do with facts. It's hard enough for us to be able to understand, and we have the gift! People who have never had their dreams wandered just don't get it."

"That's true," Gren agreed. "I'm sorry, Lawson, I don't mean to be grumpy. It's just that…we're close, I can feel it. Just not close enough."

"We'll have Winnie back soon," Lawson promised. He just wished that he felt as confident as he sounded.

Chapter Twenty-Seven

Bryce had been right, Winnie was very sore. She didn't complain, she kept reminding herself that she would be home soon. They slowed their pace slightly because of the pain, but they continued on.

"Tell me about your sister," Bryce suggested. He ached' as much as Winnie did. He figured that conversation might take their minds off it.

"She looks a lot like I do," Winnie started. "Only an older version."

"No, that's not what I meant. What's she like? You two are obviously close."

Winnie sighed. "Not as close as I'd like. She was already in school by the time I was born, so for most of the orbit she would be away. We'd have fun when Gren and Lawson would come home on break. I remember little bits and pieces of hiding or running games from when I was a kid."

"Wait," Bryce said. "You said Gren and Lawson. He spent breaks with you as well?"

"Lawson's an orphan," Winnie explained. "They were partnered their first orbit at the Learning Center, the only male/female partnering to make it all the way through the program. They've always been really close, and so Lawson spent his breaks with us. That's why I was looking forward to this vacation so much. Even though Lawson is still very much a part of Gren's life, it was going to be nice to spend a little bit of time just her and me. And Mollie of course."

"Winnie, I'm so—"

"Don't say it!" Winnie pleaded. "I know you're sorry. If it hadn't been for you, Number Two would have found someone else to help him, and I'm sure his other friends aren't as nice as you are."

"What other friends? Two can be very…difficult. I'm sure that you figured that out by now."

"Yeah, I kind of assumed it."

"This looks like a good spot for a break." Bryce sat down and Winnie sat next to him. "If you had only known him before. He has a little brother, and they used to be close. The kid drove us nuts when we were younger, always tagging along. Two liked to tease him because his brother has a very common name, while Two's name is more unique. His brother would tease back, saying that at least his was easy to remember. But it was all in fun. Then they would chase each other around. I'd come up here with them sometimes and we'd run through the woods and get lost, and not find our way back until after dark."

"You're not going to get lost now, are you?" Winnie was joking, but a small part of her was worried.

"No, I know where we're headed." Bryce took a sip of water. "It's a little bit out of the way, but I don't think that Two will realize what I'm up to."

"How far out of the way?" Winnie asked. She hadn't told Bryce that Lawson had wandered her dream. She didn't remember it all that well, just knew that he had been there, they were looking for her, and that she had somehow managed to embarrass him.

"Not too far," Bryce said. He took another sip of water. "We'd better get moving."

∘ ∘ ●◗ ∘ ∘

A unit later Winnie was beginning to think that maybe their trip was hopeless. She hated the new color of her once-white uniform. At first she had doubted it would ever be clean again, but eventually passed the time with fantasies of burning it. She had hoped that they would have run into Gren and Lawson a long time ago, and was beginning to be scared that they had missed each other. More than anything she wanted to be back at Gren's, sitting on the cot in the cramped quarters, laughing with her sister and Mollie. With every step she took, she tried to convince herself that they were closer, but it wasn't working.

Bryce noticed Winnie's mood change. "Are you okay?"

Winnie nodded. "Just tired."

"Do you want to take another break?"

"No, I'd rather keep going." Winnie took a step and her right foot sank deep into some mud. "Ewww!"

"I was just about to warn you," Bryce said. "We're near an underground stream. Watch your footing—it can be a little bit tricky around here."

Winnie took another step, her left shoe filled with water and mud. "I see what you mean."

"At least we know that Two won't be looking for us here. Who would make their way through a swamp, right?" Bryce grinned slightly at Winnie.

Winnie glanced at Bryce's feet. They were also covered.

"We'll cross here, and this will take us to the river," Bryce said.

"Oh joy, more water." Winnie hadn't meant to be sarcastic, it just slipped out.

"The river eventually runs into Lake Collins," Bryce continued. "It cuts a winding path. A path that runs directly behind the station."

"The station?" Winnie perked up. "You mean we're almost there?"

"Almost, no. Closer, yes."

"Well come on, let's get going!" Winnie picked up her pace, no longer minding the mud that was squishing between her toes.

"Winnie, watch your step!" Bryce warned loudly. "It can be a little—"

It was too late. Winnie screamed as she disappeared from view. Bryce hurried to where she had been micros earlier and peered into the hole. It was dark, but running water was visible. Bryce jumped into the opening. Water was soon over his head. He pushed himself back up to the surface. "Winnie!" he screamed.

Winnie didn't answer. She was trying desperately to keep her head above the water.

Bryce saw her downstream and realized immediately that the young girl didn't know how to swim. He pushed forward, using the current to his advantage. "I'm coming, Winnie," he called, hoping to offer some encouragement. The pack on his back was slowing him down so he wiggled out of it, not thinking if they would need anything inside of it.

Winnie continued to struggle. Her own pack weighed her down. She went under and used every ounce of strength that she had to pull herself back up. The current grabbed her and flipped her around. Her head went under again. She tried, but she just couldn't do it. Images filled her mind. She saw Gren, Lawson and her parents. Next was Mollie; the moment they met, their first night as roommates, the first time that Mollie had a strange dream, their trip to visit Gren, their playing in the park. The next thing that flashed through Winnie's mind was a closing door and the feeling of someone seizing her from behind.

"Come on, Winnie, I need your help!" Bryce had grabbed her and pushed her head back above the water. "If we do this together we can get to the side."

Winnie nodded and found more strength. She took a deep breath and started to cough.

"Shallow breaths, small amounts of air," Bryce instructed. "And let's get rid of this." Holding Winnie above the surface with one arm, he fought to remove the pack that had filled with water. Once it was gone, Winnie was able to keep her head up with a lot less difficulty. "That should be better. Hold on to me, we'll try to get to the side."

Winnie put her arms around Bryce's neck and held on as tightly as she could. She coughed several more times.

Bryce pushed hard and swam slightly against the current. He headed for the side, where the water was calmer. The underground cavern was dark, but bits of light peeked through from holes in the ground up above. Soon they were both out of the deep water and seated in a shallow pool. "Breath slowly. Are you okay?"

Winnie nodded as she coughed. "You—you saved my life. Thank you." She coughed again, but it was lessening.

"It's my fault that you're even here," Bryce replied, not

really sure what else he should say. He coughed as well. "We lost all of our supplies. We'll be following the river the rest of the way, so at least we'll have water. The river water is drinkable."

"I think I've swallowed enough water for a while," Winnie said, coughing again. "Bryce, I won't forget what you did here. I'll tell them all about it. You could have just left me, but you decided to risk your own life to save mine."

"There wasn't a choice. There was no way I was going to let you drown." Bryce coughed again.

Winnie took a deeper breath, enjoying the feeling. She grinned. "I thought you said it was an underground *stream* that led to the river."

Bryce nodded. "It is. We'll follow along the edge, and it should take us to the main river which will, in turn, take us to the station."

"If the current is that strong for a stream, I'm going to stay away from the river," Winnie said with a smile.

Chapter Twenty-Eight

"What's that sound?" Gren asked.

"What, I don't hear—"

"Lawson, shhhh!" Gren held up a hand and stopped so that she could listen. "Can't you hear that?"

Lawson shook his head. "The only thing that I can hear is the river."

"That's it!" Gren ran forward, towards the sound of rushing water.

Lawson tried to catch up. "I don't see what the big deal is."

Gren stopped at the river's bank and stared. "It's beautiful."

"Yeah," Lawson agreed, "but I still don't understand."

"The map," Gren said. "Don't you remember? If you plot where the cabin is, the path that we think they're following, and the station, the river is right there. I thought it was a little bit further out, but I've never been good at reading maps. Lawson, they'll probably be following it. We're close, I can feel it."

Lawson grinned. There was nothing that Gren wasn't good at, including reading maps. "What's that?" He pointed into a shallow part of the water. "There's something caught on that broken branch."

Gren shook her head. "Let's go see."

They carefully made their way to the edge of the water. Lawson took a step closer and his foot sank into the mud. He bent forward and grabbed a large piece of cloth. Gren took his hand and pulled him back up. "Looks like part of a bedroll," Lawson commented.

"That makes sense. Probably from a camper or something. A lot of people enjoy sleeping under the stars." Gren looked out into the water and noticed other items floating by. "There's more."

"Someone must have lost their pack, up where the current is stronger."

Gren grabbed Lawson's arm in fear. "You don't think it was Winnie, do you? She doesn't know how to swim."

"There are no signs that anyone fell into the water," Lawson said calmly. "Just their stuff. And we have no idea how long that's even been in there. It could have been caught upstream for lunar cycles and just broken free now. Don't jump to conclusions. As you said, we're close. Let's keep looking."

"Winnie!" Gren screamed with all her might. "Can you hear me? Winnie!!!"

"Winnie!" Lawson called. "Winnie!" They listened for a micro. "If they're following the river it's going to be hard to hear over the noise of the water," Lawson said. He was making an excuse for the lack of a reply.

○ ○ ○●○ ○ ○

The underground stream ran through a cave and eventually led Winnie and Bryce back outside. "There," Bryce said, pointing. "The river."

"It's beautiful," Winnie said. "And we just follow this to the station?"

"Yup." Bryce took a few quick steps forward. Something in the water caught his eye. "Look, Winnie, it's one of our packs, or rather what's left of it." The frame of the pack was lodged between two rocks. There was some torn material on the top of the frame, but all of the contents were long gone.

"What are we going to do without any supplies?" Winnie asked.

"You let me worry about it when the time comes," Bryce said.

"Wait a micro," Winnie said. She held up a handing, listening. "Did you hear that? Way off in the distance—sounds like a man's voice...calling someone."

Bryce listened for a micro. "I don't hear anything. But Winnie, we've got to be careful. It could be Two, looking for us. Maybe following the river wasn't such a good idea after all."

⋄ ⋄ ◦ ● ◦ ⋄ ⋄

"We're supposed to meet Gren and Lawson soon," Tayo reminded her partner. They were searching from the glidemobile. "We can't be too far from where they are."

"Can't we search just a little bit longer?" Mollie asked. "We're close, I know it."

"We're not going to stop searching," Calli said. "But we do need to meet up with Gren and Lawson. What if they already found Winnie? Then we could all be on our way back soon."

"I hadn't thought of that. Come on, Calli, let's park this thing and find Gren and Lawson!"

Calli glanced at Tayo and they both smiled. Mollie's enthusiasm was a good thing to see.

"Have you had any more of the dreams lately?" Tayo asked.

"None that have to do with Winnie," Mollie replied. "Not since a strange, short one. Gren told me that there was one last night that had to do with someone eating soup, but she had no idea who it was. She didn't recognize the place either. That's one of the annoying things about the dreams; they can be about pretty much anybody. Sometimes they focus on someone I know, especially if that person has been on my mind a lot, but sometimes they're random. I just want to get rid of them."

"Once we get Winnie back, we'll concentrate on finding a way to make that happen," Tayo promised.

"That looks like a good spot," Calli said, changing the subject. She steered the glidemobile to a small clearing near a drop off. "They shouldn't be too far from here."

◦ ◦ ● ◐ ● ◦ ◦

"Gren, Lawson! You guys anywhere around?" Calli called at the top of her lungs. "Gren! Lawson!"

"Gren! Lawson!" Tayo and Mollie joined in.

"Wait," Calli said, holding up her hand. "Do you hear that? We must be near the river."

"That's going to make it harder for them to hear us," Tayo observed.

"Let's go closer," Mollie said. She started to run.

"Mollie, wait! Don't get near the edge!" Calli called.

"I'll keep an eye on her," Tayo said. She knew that her partner was still a little bit wary after her fall. She ran to try to catch up with the child.

Calli walked cautiously ahead. "Gren, Lawson!" she called again.

"There they are!" Mollie pointed, turned, and ran towards the river.

"Mollie, be careful!" Calli yelled.

"I'll keep an eye on her," Tayo said again.

Soon Mollie and Tayo had caught up with Gren and

Lawson. "Watch your step, kid," Lawson warned. "There's quite a drop off here."

"Just a unit ago we were walking right next to the river but now; look at that cliff!" Gren added.

Mollie carefully walked to the edge and peered over. "The river is really beautiful. This is the first one that I've ever seen." She looked at Lawson. "What's that?"

Lawson held up the torn piece of bedroll. "This? It's nothing. We just found it floating in the water."

Mollie's face grew worried. "You think it has something to do with Winnie, don't you."

"No," Gren said a little bit too quickly. "As you said, the river is beautiful. It didn't seem right to just leave it in the water." She glanced over at Calli, who had just joined them. "Calli, what happened? Are you okay?"

Calli reached up and touched her face. "This? It's nothing. I just took a bad step. Does it look that bad?"

"No," Gren said. She lowered her voice. "It's just that—in the dream that Mollie had, you had a cut on your face. I had totally forgotten about that until now."

Tayo grinned at her partner. "She's just worried that she'll look bad when we see Sham again."

"I am not! I just don't want—" Calli was interrupted by a scream.

"Gren!!!"

Gren turned around. "Winnie!" She rushed forward and threw her arms around her sister. She held her tightly, not wanting to ever let go. "Winnie, I've been so worried about you." The tears fell freely down Gren's face.

"I'm fine," Winnie said. She held her sister for several micros before wiggling away. She then embraced Lawson, Calli, Tayo, and finally Mollie. "Calli, what happened to your face?"

Calli touched the cut again. She looked at Gren. "You told me it didn't look that bad."

"It doesn't," Tayo said with a sigh.

Winnie walked over to the side. "Hey everybody, this is Bryce. He's my friend. I never would have escaped without him, and that's exactly what I plan on telling the System Workers. Bryce, this is—" she pointed as she spoke, "—Gren, Lawson, Tayo, Calli and Mollie."

Bryce seemed extremely uncomfortable. "Listen, everyone, I'm sorry about—"

"Just ignore him when he apologizes, he does it a lot. Gren, he saved my life. I almost drowned, but he risked his own life to save me."

Gren looked at Bryce. "Thank you."

"It shouldn't have been necessary. If I hadn't—"

Winnie sighed loudly. "I keep trying to tell you that if it hadn't been you, Two would have found someone else to help him, someone who wouldn't have been so nice."

"You still don't know Two's name?" Lawson asked.

"No, Lawson, but you do." Everyone turned around, surprised that Winnie's main kidnapper had snuck up on the group. He held something in his hands.

Chapter Twenty-Nine

"Thaddeus?" Lawson wasn't even sure what to say. "What do you have to do with any of this?"

"You know him?" Calli asked.

"He's an Associate Wanderer," Lawson explained. "He works for Haas."

"Haas!" Thaddeus repeated with a laugh. "That cheapskate. You're right, I 'work' for Haas, being paid what I'm *worth* by him is certainly another story. Gren, prove me right about how cheap he is. What's your payback percentage?"

Gren instinctively moved in front of Winnie, who was already holding Mollie tightly. "Twenty-five percent. Why?"

Thaddeus laughed. "Twenty-five? Wow, you two are bigger suckers than I thought. Grey's is only ten."

"You know Grey?" Lawson asked.

Thaddeus laughed again. "Of course I know Grey. He's my brother. He's the one who told me that Mollie here," he pointed to Winnie, "has been having premonition dreams. He overheard those two idiots, Sham and Titus, talking to Cassidy. Grey told me their whole conversation. He just didn't realize that I would come up with a plan to use that information."

"Thad," Bryce said slowly, "that's not Mollie. The girl we grabbed is Winnie, Gren's little sister."

"Even better," Thaddeus said. "A chance to make Gren's life

miserable, after what she's done to mine."

"What did I ever do to you?" Gren asked.

Thaddeus laughed a third time. "Do you know how long I tried to get Haas to agree to take Grey on as an apprentice? I wanted to be able to keep an eye on my little brother. He's a loner, he doesn't make friends easily, and I thought it would be good for him if I kept him close. But no, Haas doesn't take apprentices. So finally I was able to talk Cassidy into hiring him, at least he'd be nearby. Then, all of a sudden, Haas had taken on not one, but two apprentices. The great Gren and Lawson, 'the only male/female partnering to ever make it all the way through the Learning Center'."

"You knew about that?" Lawson asked.

Thaddeus looked disgusted. "*Every* Wanderer out there knows about that. Haas was almost salivating to get the two of you. To your faces he makes it seem like you're such a bother, but you should hear the way he talks to Aribella and me. 'Lawson is making great progress—he has such a way with the kids. He's going to be great. Gren is the most talented Wanderer that I've ever seen. But she's too settled. I need to be hard on her, push her to go further. She has so much natural ability that if she maximizes her potential she could revolutionize wandering.' Hearing Haas drone on and on about the two of you just makes me sick. Ever since you started in his practice he's been harder on the rest of us, keeps telling us that we need to step up to your level. I've been wandering for orbits, and I'm supposed to emulate *you*? Don't make me sick."

"I'm sorry, Thaddeus," Gren said. "I never knew any of this."

"It doesn't matter," Thaddeus said. "It's all over anyway."

He turned on the device that he was holding and the lights started flashing.

Gren immediately recognized the gadget from Mollie's dream.

"Thad, no," Bryce said. "It's over now. We can just let them go."

"So you can turn me in to the System Workers? I wandered a dream that Mollie, or Winnie, or whatever her name is, had. She told Lawson that you plan on turning me in. Is that true, my *friend*?"

"Hey, I was just trying to get the kid to trust me," Bryce said. "We had the wrong one! I figured I'd get her back home, and then we'd disappear. I wasn't going to tell anyone anything, Thad. Why do you think I never told her your name?"

"Nice try, Bryce." Thaddeus laughed, and started walking forwards. He pointed the device towards Bryce and pressed a button.

"Nooo!" Winnie screamed as Bryce fell to the ground.

"Don't worry, Mollie...Winnie...whatever your name is. He's just stunned. He should be out for a while, but there's no permanent damage. Although he could have broken a bone or something as he fell, I guess that's possible. Now, the rest of you, come with me. Unless, of course, you'd like to end up like my *best friend* there."

Lawson took a slight step forward, guarding Gren. "We don't have to do anything that you—"

Thaddeus pressed the button again and Lawson fell to the ground. "Anybody else?"

Gren bent down and checked on Lawson. "He's breathing; he's just knocked out."

"That was very chivalrous of him, but also foolish," Thaddeus said. He slowly inched his way closer to the group. "Does Haas know about you two? He has a very strict rule about inter-office dating."

Gren ignored the comment. "What is it you want from us?"

"What I want, Gren," Thaddeus started slowly, "is for you to shut up and do what I tell you." He rushed forward, grabbed Winnie, and held her around the neck with one arm. "Stunning the kid won't kill her, but snapping her neck will. Now everybody, we're going to head out to that glidemobile back there." He laughed again. "Everybody who hasn't been stunned, that is. I'll deal with them later."

Calli and Tayo took Mollie's hands and allowed her to walk between them. Gren tried to stay back, near Winnie, but Thaddeus ordered her in front of him. She was upset with herself, checking on Lawson had given Thaddeus the opportunity to grab Winnie. It wasn't far to Calli's glidemobile. A black one was nearby.

"Whose vehicle is it?" Thaddeus asked.

"Mine, why?" Calli asked.

"Get in," Thaddeus ordered. "Just don't turn it on. The two of you as well." He motioned towards Tayo and Mollie.

"But—" The word was barely out of Mollie's mouth when Thaddeus tightened his grip around Winnie's neck. "Okay."

As soon as Calli, Tayo and Mollie were all inside the glidemobile, Thaddeus raised his free arm and stunned the three of them. They all slumped down.

"What are you doing?" Winnie asked, struggling.

"I have to make it look like an accident, don't I?"

"Make what look like an accident?" Gren dreaded the reply.

Thaddeus shook his head. "Gren, I thought that you were supposed to be a smart one. Your deaths, of course. It's quite simple, really. After I've stunned you and your annoying little sister, I'll place your sleeping bodies in the glidemobile as well. I'll drag Lawson over here and throw him in. Then I'll turn the glidemobile on...you saw that drop off over towards the river. The crash will kill all of you instantly."

Winnie continued to struggle. "What about Bryce? No one will believe that he was in the glidemobile with us."

"Ah, yes, my best friend, who wanted to turn me in. That's also very simple. I plan on hitting him with my own glidemobile, then dumping him in the river. The System Workers will believe that *you* hit him, and that's why you lost control. They'll also believe that he was the one responsible for the kidnapping."

"The System Workers must realize that two people were involved," Gren said.

"But I have an alibi. I've been at work every rotation since your sister went missing. I've been working extra units since Haas had his accident. Besides, Gren, you know how the System Workers are. They'll base their case on facts, and the only conclusion that they'll be able to come to is that Bryce worked alone. They'll assume that he grabbed the kid for ransom. They'll be more than happy to close the case, even if it did result in several deaths. They'll just blame Bryce and forget all about the details."

"You're not going to get away with this," Gren stated.

Winnie pulled back her elbow and rammed it hard into Thaddeus' stomach. Reflexively, he let go.

"Run, Winnie, run!" Gren screamed.

Thaddeus immediately used the device to stun Gren. Winnie took one quick look back and saw her sister fall to the ground. Winnie ran as fast as she could, hoping to be able to hide in the woods. Thaddeus tried to stun her but she was too far away. Winnie knew that she had to lead him away, try to buy some time. It was the only chance that they had.

· · · ● ◉ ● · · ·

Winnie wasn't sure what she should do. She didn't want to be too far from where Gren and her friends had been stunned, but she didn't want to stick too close because she knew that Thaddeus was looking for her. If he caught her it would be easier for him to implement his plan; if her body was on the outside of the glidemobile with Bryce's the System Workers would probably believe that he was the lone kidnapper and that they were all the victims of a glidemobile accident. Winnie's first instinct was to run as far away as possible, just keep going, but she tried instead to think logically. The last thing that she needed was to get lost. The sky was growing dark, a storm was moving in.

"Win...nie," Thaddeus called, an insincere quality in his voice. "Come on, girl, just come out. You know that I'm not really going to hurt you. The whole time that you were with me, did I ever do anything to scare you? Did I threaten you in any way? Of course not! I'm not going to hurt you, and I'm not going to hurt your friends. We'll work something out. How about this—you come out now, and we'll just forget about the whole thing? You can go home with your sister, as soon as she wakes up, and I'll take Bryce and we'll disappear. You'll never see us again."

Winnie wanted to believe that Thaddeus' offer was genuine,

but she knew better. Things couldn't go back to the way that they were before. Gren and Lawson worked with Thaddeus, were they just supposed to ignore him? It made no sense. As she hid behind a tree, she could see Thaddeus searching for her. At least he was heading in the wrong direction.

"Win...nie," Thaddeus called again. The wind was picking up, and there was a loud clap of thunder. "It's going to storm. You don't want to be out here in a storm, do you? A young girl like you...you must hate the thunder. I know I did when I was your age. Out here in the woods, with all these trees...which one do you think the lightning will hit first? Or maybe it will just strike Gren. She *is* lying out in the open, not a great place to be during a storm."

Winnie felt something wet on her face. She wasn't sure if it was a tear or a raindrop, but as the rain started to fall she realized that it was probably both. Quietly she moved out of her hiding place to look for another. The rain poured down and there was another clap of thunder. It sounded as if the storm was right on top of them. At least the sound of the rain made it more difficult to hear Thaddeus. A lightning strike lit up a group of trees, showing Winnie a good place to hide.

"Oh come on, Winnie!" Thaddeus yelled. "Enough of this. Just get out here, now! If you don't, well, then I think I'll just head back and take care of Gren instead. Is that what you want? You want to be responsible for your sister's death? I tried to reason with you, I gave you an opportunity to just forget about everything, but did you listen to me? So that's it, Winnie. Gren's death will be on *your* head."

As lightning lit up the sky again Winnie could see that Thaddeus had changed directions. He appeared to be heading back towards Calli's glidemobile.

"Tell you what, Winnie," Thaddeus continued as he walked. "I'm going to kill them all, one by one, until you show yourself to me. I'll start with Gren, and then move on to that other kid." He paused. "Wait a micro. Is *that* Mollie? Is she the one who is really having the premonition dreams? I just may let her live, go back to my original plan with her. I'll just keep mixing tonics until I get the right combination. Who cares if it's all untested?"

Winnie snuck out of her hiding place and followed Thaddeus at a distance. The rain and thunder drowned out the sound of her footsteps. She didn't know what to do; she just wanted to keep him in her sights. Maybe Bryce would wake up soon. He was the first one stunned—he should be the first to wake up. She knew that she needed help, she couldn't save everyone alone. As long as they were near the glidemobile, she had a little bit of hope. She found a group of young trees growing nearby and hid behind them. She kept her eyes on Bryce, sleeping on the ground, and listened to Thaddeus' constant chatter to keep track of his position.

Another lightning strike lit up the sky. After the thunder, everything grew eerily quiet. Thaddeus had stopped his barrage. Winnie looked around; she couldn't see him anywhere. She moved slightly away from her hiding place to get a better look. It was a mistake.

Chapter Thirty

Winnie struggled against the arm that was once again around her neck. "Let go of me!" she screamed.

Thaddeus laughed. "Not this time. You've been *way* more trouble than you're worth and I'm going to make you pay for all the problems that you've caused me."

"All the problems that I've caused you? This whole thing is your sick plan! I was *supposed* be spending a nice, quiet break with my sister and my best friend, but you ruined everything!"

"I'm about to ruin a whole lot more," Thaddeus said. "Namely, your entire life. Or what's left of it."

Thaddeus dragged Winnie back towards the glidemobile. Winnie struggled the entire time. She almost wiggled herself free, until Thaddeus used his other arm to help hold her. The stunning device slipped out of his wet hand and fell to the ground. With a burst of strength, Winnie stepped firmly on it and it broke into two pieces.

"Now look what you've done!" Thaddeus screamed. He tightened his grip so that Winnie could hardly breathe. "I made that myself. I worked on it for over two orbits! You're really going to pay now…"

Winnie pulled back her elbow and hit Thaddeus hard in the stomach. He let go and she ran away from him, but she soon realized that there was no place to go. The glidemobiles blocked one way; she couldn't make it around them. Thaddeus was guarding where they had just been. The only choice was heading closer towards the river, but she knew that there was a drop off. Thaddeus started walking closer, as if trying to force her in that direction. Winnie decided that if she were going to die she would rather it be by falling over a cliff than by strangulation. She also thought that just maybe she would have a chance to run away, as long as she kept as much distance between Thaddeus and herself as possible.

There was a groan; Bryce was starting to wake up. Winnie rushed to his side, she was saved! "Bryce," she said, shaking his shoulder. "Come on, Bryce, wake up."

Bryce stretched and sat up. "Winnie? Where are we? What's going on?"

Winnie pulled on his arm to try to get him to his feet. "Don't you remember? Thaddeus is about to kill all of us unless you get up now!"

Thaddeus stood and watched with an amused look on his face.

Bryce rubbed the back of his head as he stood up stood up. "Oh, yeah. Hey, Thad, you stunned me! That wasn't part of the plan."

"Neither was you taking off with the kid."

"We had the wrong one!" Bryce exclaimed. "It didn't make much sense to keep her. I figured that if I'd get her to trust me and get her home, she'd be really grateful and not press charges. She never saw your face and I didn't give you up, Thad. Neither one of us would have ended up in a Labor Camp. Everything was fine until you came looking for us. But I've been on your side all along. We're friends; you should know that I wouldn't betray you."

Thaddeus shook his head. "If you mean what you say—"

Bryce knew what Thaddeus wanted. He grabbed Winnie from behind and held her arms down.

Winnie struggled but couldn't get away. "Bryce, I thought you were on my side. I thought you were going to help!"

"Sorry, Winnie," Bryce said.

○ ○ ○●○ ○ ○

Still holding Winnie, Bryce started to move towards the glidemobile. Thaddeus was right beside them. "You'd better hurry, Thad," Bryce said. "If I woke up this quickly the effects of the stun will probably wear off everyone else soon."

"Yeah, you're right," Thaddeus replied. He grabbed Lawson by the feet and dragged him towards the glidemobile. "Hey, aren't you going to help? We'll just knock the kid out and throw her in too."

"You don't want to do that, Thad," Bryce said. "You don't want them finding her with any signs of extra injuries. I assume that you're trying to make this look like an accident."

"Yeah. Like they found her but then just lost control of the glidemobile and crashed. But knock her out! They'll think that she hurt herself in the accident."

"The System Workers are so overworked these rotations that they'll close the case, assume that Winnie had run away instead of being kidnapped, and then her sister found her. But an extra bump on the head would be too suspicious." Bryce dragged Winnie towards the far side of the glidemobile, away from Thaddeus. "We're going to sit down for a hundred. I think it's going to take a little while for the stun to wear off fully. I still can't believe that you did that!"

"You blame me?" Thaddeus asked.

"I would never have doubted your friendship." Bryce sat down, pulling Winnie down with him.

Winnie continued to struggle. It didn't feel to her like Bryce was trying to wear off the effects of a stun, he was holding her tightly. "I trusted you," she said, hatred and fear in her voice.

"Shhh," Bryce whispered in Winnie's ear. "I'm on your side. Continue to fight against me, and when I let go, head towards the road. It shouldn't be too far. Run as fast as you can, and wave down the first glidemobile that you see. Have them take you to the station and bring back the System Workers. I'll hold Thad off here. You got it?"

Winnie nodded slightly. She tried not to grin. "I knew you had to still be on my side."

"I won't let him hurt you or any of your friends. I promise."

"What are you two whispering about?" Thaddeus called.

Bryce laughed. "You should hear the names this kid is calling you, Thad! I bet she doesn't even know what half of them mean."

"I do too," Winnie yelled. She continued to make it look like she was trying to get away. "And I mean every one of them."

Thaddeus had dragged Lawson by his feet to the glidemobile and bent down to pick him up. "I still think we should just knock her out." Thaddeus placed Lawson inside and busied himself with adjusting Lawson's unconscious body to make it look like he was sitting normally.

Bryce decided that the time was right. "Now's your chance, go!" He let go of Winnie and she took off as fast as she could. He watched as Winnie disappeared from sight. He stood up and walked towards the glidemobile. "It's over, Thad. Winnie's gone to get help. There's no reason to hurt anyone any further. You're just making things worse for both of us."

Thaddeus stared towards the road. He had been so busy with Lawson that he hadn't even realized that Winnie was gone. "Traitor," was all that he had to say.

"I'm not a traitor," Bryce said, "but I'm not a kidnapper either! How did I ever let you talk me into this ridiculous scheme?"

"It wasn't that hard," Thaddeus reminded him. "Look at you. You act like you're the good one in all of this and that I'm pure evil or something. But all I had to do was mention a financial reward and your so-called morals went flying right out the window."

"You're right," Bryce said. "I did it for the money. But at least I came around and realized that what we were doing was wrong."

Thaddeus laughed. "Don't give me that. The only reason you had your little change of heart was because we had the wrong kid. If we had the right one and we were able to make a profit off her dreams, you wouldn't have let her go. You never had a problem with any of it when you thought we were going to get rich off of her."

Bryce stood silently for a micro. "You're right," he said at last. "With the initial plan I'm no better than you are in all of this. But at least I didn't hurt anybody."

"Well maybe you should have." Thaddeus took a swing at Bryce and caught him off guard, hitting him firmly in the stomach. Bryce doubled over in pain and didn't even notice that Thaddeus was going for the cross blow. One more hit firmly on Bryce's jaw caused him to fall to the ground, unconscious again. "My friend," Thaddeus mumbled.

Winnie ran with everything that she had. Soon she had made it to the road. She was worried that no one would come by in time. Bryce had told her that it wasn't a heavily traveled route, and she hoped and prayed that someone would be there quickly. She was grateful that the rain was starting to subside, the storm was passing.

As she bent over to catch her breath, Winnie heard a sound. A glidemobile was approaching! She stood in the middle of the road and waved her arms. She knew that they could run her over but she was desperate. When it was obvious that they weren't even about to slow down she jumped out of the way.

A hundred later she heard a similar sound. Winnie went back into the road and waved her arms again.

"Look at that!" Grey said, pointing. "There's some kid in the middle of the road."

"That's not some kid, that's Winnie!" Titus exclaimed. "Sham, slow down. Gren would kill us if we ended up running her over, especially after everything she's been through."

Sham steered the glidemobile to the side of the road. "Hey kid," he called, "need a ride?"

Titus immediately jumped out and Winnie ran into his arms. She started to cry. "He's going to kill them," she mumbled.

"Who?" Titus asked. "And where are they?"

Winnie took a step back and wiped her eyes. "Thaddeus." She pointed. "He's down that way, not too far. He has Gren and Mollie and everybody else, and he's going to crash their glidemobile. I got away to get help."

Grey stepped out of the glidemobile and stood next to Titus.

"Sham should take her to get the System Workers. You and I will confront my brother."

"But I—" Sham protested from inside the glidemobile.

"Grey's right," Titus said. "We can't waste any time, you're already driving. We need to get Winnie out of here. Plus you and Grey don't exactly get along, let alone work well together." Titus helped Winnie into the vehicle.

Sham didn't seem happy about it but nodded in acceptance.

Winnie stared at Titus. "What happened to your face?" she asked him.

"I'll tell you later. How far up the road are they?"

Winnie pointed again. "Not too far. You should be able to see the black glidemobile on the left, tucked behind a tree."

"We'll find him," Titus promised. He looked at Grey, who nodded.

Chapter Thirty-One

Thaddeus dumped Gren into the glidemobile then wiped the sweat off his forehead. "One more," he said out loud, "then I'm going for the brat." He took a deep breath before bending over Bryce.

"Thad, what's going on?"

"Grey?" Thaddeus looked surprised. "What are you doing here?"

"I'm looking for you." Grey took a few steps towards his brother. "I heard all kinds of terrible things about you, Thad, but I didn't want to believe them."

"Heard from who?"

"Sham and Titus."

Thaddeus laughed. "You're going to believe those two? All you've ever done is complain about them; tell me how annoying they are, how they think they're better than everyone else. And now they think they know...what? Come on, Grey, I'm your brother. You're going to believe them over me?"

Grey shook his head. "It's hard not to believe them when I can clearly see what's going on. We found Gren's sister, Thad. Sham and Titus have taken her to get help. The System Workers will be here in a few hundreds."

"Then we'd better move fast. Hey, I have an idea. We'll get both glidemobiles out of here, that way when the System

Workers come they won't find anything. We'll get rid of them somewhere else. We'll...we'll...we'll dump them all in a cabin and burn it down! That would work. That old abandoned one near ours. We'll make it look like they were caught in the storm and sought shelter, but then it was hit by lightning. But come on, Grey, we need to move fast. They're going to start waking up soon."

Grey walked the last few steps towards his brother. "I'm not going to help you murder anyone."

"Murder? That's such a harsh word. I prefer to think of it as wrapping up loose ends."

"What's happened to you, Thad? I never thought that you'd stoop to such a level. I'm not going to be a part of it."

Thaddeus was visibly hurt. "Everything I've done has been for you—to give you a better life—and now you're standing here, *judging* me? What are you going to do, Grey? Turn me over to the System Workers?"

"If I have to."

"Why you little..." Thaddeus rushed towards his brother. "I'm not going to spend the rest of my life in the Labor Camps because of you." He took a swing at Grey, which landed cleanly on his jaw.

Grey took a step back, knowing that his brother could easily beat him in a fight. "It's not because of me; it's because of what you've done. Kidnapping a little girl for profit? Come on, Thad!"

"You're the one who told me about her."

"I asked you a question! I was curious if you had heard about Premonition Dreaming. That's all."

"You had to come to me, because those two buffoons that

you apprentice with were totally ignoring you. They wouldn't come to you, share their question with you. Would it have killed them to talk with you a little bit, try to become your friend? But no, they just walk around, acting like they're better than everyone else."

Grey shook his head. "You're changing the subject, Thad."

"That's because I don't want to fight you. You're my little brother, Grey. After Mom and Dad died, I raised you. I've always taken care of you. But I do *one little thing* that you don't agree with, and suddenly you think you're better than I am."

"'One little thing'?" Grey repeated. "Thad, you're loading people into a glidemobile and talking about killing them all in a fire!"

"Yup. Come on, Grey, we need to hurry."

Grey shook his head in disbelief. "You're crazy."

"Crazy?" Thaddeus stared at his brother, his anger growing. "Crazy? You're a stinking traitor! Whatever happened to family loyalty! I sacrificed *everything* for you, and now you're standing there, judging me?" Thaddeus slapped Grey in the face.

"I'm not going to fight you, Thad."

"Then stay out of my way, and let me finish what I was doing." Thaddeus started to move back towards the glidemobile.

Grey, not knowing what else to do, ran towards his brother and jumped on his back. He held on tight.

Thaddeus twirled around in a circle and tried to shake Grey off. "You're not going to stop me."

"No, just stall you until the System Workers get here." Grey put his hand over Thaddeus' eyes. Thaddeus lost balance and they both fell to the ground. Thaddeus landed on top of his brother and used it to his advantage. One more hard punch to the jaw and Grey moaned in pain.

"It serves you right." Thaddeus stood up and brushed himself off. "Don't worry, Grey, I'm not going to include you with the rest of them. I'll at least let you live."

Grey pulled himself up slightly. "My leg, Thad. I think it's broken. It gave out under me when I fell."

"It serves you right," Thaddeus repeated. "Look, I'll help you to my glidemobile when I'm done here."

"Which is now!" Seemingly out of nowhere, Titus had appeared. He hit Thaddeus hard in the stomach.

Thaddeus grabbed a fallen branch and swung it at Titus. He hit him once, ripping his shirt. Titus grasped the other end of the branch and held on. It broke in two. They each threw down the piece in their hands. Thaddeus tried to strike Titus, but Titus ducked. Thaddeus took advantage of Titus' new body position and struck him firmly on his already injured eye.

Titus ignored the pain and returned the blow. Acting quickly, he hit Thaddeus on the jaw, in the stomach for a second time, then again on his jaw. Thaddeus staggered a bit. Titus remembered what Sham had done previously with Grey and thumped Thaddeus soundly on the top of his head. Thaddeus howled with pain. Titus pulled back his arm for one more blow. That was all it took. Thaddeus fell in the mud, defeated.

"Finally!" Titus exclaimed. "I'm finally not the one who ends up on the ground!" He took the repair kit out of the back of the glidemobile, removed the wiring tape, and used it to tie Thaddeus' hands behind his back. "Finally."

"I should be the one to say 'finally'," Grey said, grimacing. "What took you so long?"

"You told me that you could handle it," Titus replied. He started to check everyone in the glidemobile. "That I should wait until the last micro." His friends were all breathing and seemed to be fine. "Are you okay?"

"I think my leg is broken. I fell on it at a weird angle. But I'll be fine. Listen, Titus, about what Thad said about you and Sham…"

Titus shook his head. "No, don't worry about it. Sham and I have been way too hard on you. I realize that now, and I'm sorry. Maybe if we had all tried to get along sooner, none of this would have happened. What do you think, should we try to start over?" Titus bent over and held out his hand.

Grey shook it. "Sounds good."

"Don't listen to him, Grey." Thaddeus' voice was weak but authoritative. "He's just going to make fun of you behind your back, like he's always done. I'm the only one you can trust."

"Ignore him," Grey said. "That's what I'm going to do from now on."

There was a slight moan heard from the glidemobile. Titus went over to check; Lawson was waking up. "Titus? What's going on? And what am I doing in the glidemobile?"

"What do you remember?" Titus asked.

Lawson rubbed his eyes. He then pulled himself outside. "I was with Gren and she…holy splarsh, is Gren okay?"

"Gren's fine," Titus said. "Everyone is."

"Just stunned," Grey added. "Like you were."

Lawson looked confused. "What's he doing here?"

"Without Grey's help, Sham and I never would have found you," Titus explained.

Lawson looked around. "Where *is* Sham? And Winnie?

Don't tell me that she's missing again!"

Titus shook his head. "They went to get help. The System Workers should be here any micro. It's over, Lawson."

Another groan came from inside the glidemobile. Gren moved slightly. "Lawson?"

Lawson grinned. "I knew it! I'm the first thing on her mind when she wakes up."

Chapter Thirty-Two

That evening everyone gathered in the guys' dwelling. Grey had been invited; his leg was elevated and in a cast. Tayo had taken it upon herself to watch over him, to make sure that he was comfortable. Cassidy was there as well.

"When no one was there we decided to spend the night in Grey's cabin," Sham explained. Although he didn't mention it, he was painfully aware of the fact that he was the only one from their adventure that didn't have at least one visible bruise or cut. "We thought that maybe Thaddeus would come back, and Grey could talk some sense into him. We were sure that Cassidy was going to think that we stole her glidemobile."

Cassidy laughed. "The thought had crossed my mind."

"When Thad didn't return I was pretty sure that he had headed back to his place, and I knew what he wanted," Grey added. "He had bragged to me not that long ago that he had invented some electrical thing that could knock people out without hurting them. I'm just glad that he didn't already have it with him at the cabin. I guess that he didn't think that one young girl would give him so much trouble."

"He obviously underestimated my little sister," Gren said. Winnie was sitting next to her, squirming to get a little more space but Gren didn't seem to want to let her go.

"And her friends," Cassidy added.

Sham looked at Calli. "You know, you look terrible."

"Says the only one who came out of this unscathed," Calli replied.

"Hey, I brought the System Workers!" Sham argued. "I wanted to go back, but someone had to bring help! Plus I needed to make sure that Winnie was safe."

Calli grinned. "Poke." She moved away quickly to make sure that Sham couldn't return it.

"So what's going to happen to Bryce?" Winnie asked.

"He's in the Medical Center right now with a mild concussion, but he's going to be fine," Gren explained. "The System Workers told me that they're going to take what you told them into account, how he helped you, but he's probably going to spend an orbit or two in the Labor Camps. It would have been a lot worse for him if he hadn't helped."

"Can we visit him?" Winnie asked. "I really like him, and I want him to know that I'm not holding anything against him. He saved my life more than once."

Gren held Winnie even closer. "We'll see."

"Thad's being held for mental observation," Grey said. "They told me at the Medical Center, after they worked on my leg, that he flipped out. He kept screaming about a better life and family loyalty. So he'll either spend his time at the Institute or in the Labor Camps, but either way he's not going to be bothering any of you again." He sighed. "All these orbits he's been taking care of me and now I'm responsible for making decisions for him. They're also going to remove the gift of wandering."

"Can't chance him wandering in the Labor Camps," Titus

said. He and Grey glanced at each other. They seemed to have found some sort of mutual respect.

"Oh, I almost forgot," Cassidy said. She pulled something out of her bag. "Gren, you might want to read this. It will tell you what to do. I have no doubt that you'll be able to pull it off." She stood up, handed a crumpled paper to Gren, and walked towards the door. "My glidemobile and I have to go home." She laughed. "I still can't believe that you thought that it was my husband."

Gren waited until Cassidy was gone before looking at the paper. She stared at it for several micros.

"What is it?" Lawson asked.

"It's an article about premonition dreams, and how to remove them."

Mollie perked up. "Can we do it? Can we remove those dreams for good?"

Gren smiled as she read. "It's so simple that it's brilliant. Yes, Mollie, I think that we can do it."

A unit later, all the girls were back at Gren's place. Mollie was too excited to sleep, so Gren tried a different approach. "Lie back," she instructed, "and close your eyes. Concentrate only on my voice. Take deep breaths, and imagine yourself the most comfortable that you've ever been. All of life's difficulties have been washed away; all you have to do is drift off to sleep. You're doing well. Relax, and count slowly in your mind backwards from one hundred. When you reach one, allow yourself to dream. But listen only to me; pay no attention to the dream around you."

Mollie was holding onto Winnie as tightly as she could. Thaddeus was coming towards them, pointing something at them. He raised it higher…

"No!" Gren's voice was stern. "This is not happening, and you are not to dream about it right now. Look straight ahead, and listen to me."

"Okay." Mollie's voice in the dream was shaking. Thaddeus disappeared, but Mollie continued to hold onto Winnie.

"Winnie can stay," Gren's voice said. It had softened, but was still in control. "You are to listen to me. There will be no more premonition dreams. You are *not* allowed to have any more dreams from the future. Any time that such a dream is about to form, it will turn into your favorite shade of blue. That is all that your mind will allow to materialize."

"Just blue?"

"It will be like someone poured blue paint on the dream, covering everything," Gren's voice explained. "You won't even be curious about what might be going on behind the paint; you'll just enjoy seeing the blue. Do you understand?"

Mollie nodded. "I think I can do that."

"Don't think, just do it."

"Okay."

"The dreams will lessen over time," Gren's voice continued. "Eventually they will go away all together. You don't have to worry about them anymore."

"What if I want them to come back?" Mollie asked.

"You won't want them to," Gren's voice said. "Anytime that you think that you might want them again, you'll remember that people aren't supposed to know the future. Now repeat after me. 'I will not allow myself to dream about the future ever again.'"

"I will not allow myself to dream about the future ever again."

"Any dream that might have come true will be covered with blue."

"Any dream that might have come true will be covered with blue."

"Those dreams will go away."

"Those dreams will go away."

"The only dreams that I'm allowed are the same type that everyone else has."

"The only dreams that I'm allowed are the same type that everyone else has."

"Good-bye premonition dreams."

"Good-bye premonition dreams."

"Well done. Now I want you to start counting backwards from one hundred again. When you reach one, you will wake up. You won't remember what just happened, but the premonition dreams will be gone."

· ◦ ◉ ● ◉ ◦ ◦

Mollie sat up and looked at Gren. "What happened? I don't remember anything. Did it work?"

"You did really well, Mollie," Gren said. "We'll know for sure in a few rotations, but I think that it worked."

Chapter Thirty-Three

"It's only been a few rotations, but so far so good." Gren was holding Lawson's hand as they walked to work. It was their first rotation back, Haas had just returned.

"Have there been any signs at all of the dreams?" Lawson asked.

"Winnie woke me up last night. Mollie was sitting up in bed, the same way she always did when she had the dreams. I wandered, silently, and all I saw was blue. So it seems to be working."

Lawson chuckled. "Such a simple solution."

Gren nodded. "A lot of problems in life can be solved by simple solutions. We just need to take the time to look for them."

"So philosophical!" Lawson said, laughing.

"Maybe I'm just trying to convince myself," Gren said. "I'm not looking forward to returning to work."

"Me either. You think Haas is going to blame us for losing one of his Associate Wanderers?"

"Blame *me* is more like it." Gren sighed. "I'm the one who can't do anything right by him."

"Oh, I almost forgot," Lawson said, purposely changing the subject. "Grey stopped by again last night. Thaddeus had just had the gift removed. Grey was there, he said it was really hard to watch. His brother has been declared competent and is being transferred to a Labor Camp this morning."

"I hope it's not the same one that Bryce is at. Somehow I don't think that those two will stay friends, especially once Thaddeus finds out that Bryce was sentenced to only two orbits."

"According to Grey, his brother is being sent fairly far away. Bryce is serving his time not too far from here, so it won't be the same one."

Gren smiled. "Grey seems to be spending a lot of time at your place lately."

Lawson nodded. "Yeah, he and Titus are getting along really well. I think Sham is jealous; he keeps looking at the crutches as Grey hobbles by like he's getting ideas."

"He wouldn't."

Lawson laughed. "There was a time when I thought that maybe he would, but Titus has gained so much confidence after fighting off Thaddeus that Sham would have to deal with him as well."

Gren stopped walking and stared at the building in front of them. "Might as well get this over with."

◦ ◦ ●●● ◦ ◦

A young girl sat by herself in the middle of the woods, crying. She buried her head in her lap and sobbed openly. "I—want—my—Mommy!" The child was having a difficult time catching her breath.

Gren's voice was smooth and calming, and she kept things in control. "Your mother is looking for you. You need to find her. Stand up and—"

"No!" the girl insisted. She kept her head down. "I don't

want to stand up."

"Your mother is looking for you," Gren's voice repeated, "but you have to help her. Stand up, and walk towards the bridge. You'll see her on the other side."

"But..."

"Do it now. You know that it's what you want to do. You want to find her so that she can take you home. Stand up, now."

"Okay." The girl stood up and took a few steps forward towards the bridge. "You're right, there she is! Mommy!" The child ran forward and into the arms of the woman who was waiting for her.

Everything went dark.

○ ○ ○●○ ○ ○

"Somebody's been practicing." Haas had crutches nearby, although the rest of the signs of his accident had faded.

"Yes, Sir, I have," Gren replied. Lawson sat next to her.

Haas almost smiled. "It shows. Your confidence is starting to come through. You didn't allow the child in the simulation to take over, you kept control all along. Good work, Gren."

Gren was surprised. "Thank you, Sir."

"I'm going to have to reorganize the structure of things around here, especially after the unexpected loss of one of my Associate Wanderers, so I'm going to step both of you up a bit. Gren, you'll observe, starting the rotation after tomorrow, and you'll both be doing some practice wandering by the end of the lunar cycle."

"Thank you, Sir," Gren repeated.

Haas sat back and adjusted the position of his injured leg. "I know I've been hard on you, Gren. From what Thaddeus said when I removed the gift I've been hard on everyone. However, the reason with you is simple. You have a lot of potential, even more than I expected after Ladinda's glowing recommendation. But you can't make a living on potential. Wandering is one percent gift, ninety-nine percent hard work. It's not that you weren't trying, because you were. But with your talent you're going to end up with some really tough cases, and it's my job to make sure that you're prepared."

Gren sat there, stunned by what she had just heard.

"Excuse me, Sir," Lawson said. "You're the one who removed the gift from Thaddeus?"

"I'm one of only two in this area who is licensed to remove it," Haas replied. "Ladinda is the other. It's not a pretty sight. Thaddeus had a lot to say about both of you and about me. He also kept calling his brother and someone named Bryce a traitor."

"Sir…we…" Lawson started.

Haas held up a hand. "I don't want to know. I've read the reports from the System Workers, so I know the basics of what happened. I'm sorry, Gren, that it involved your sister. Thaddeus was a very good Wanderer, but he was in too much of a hurry. That's a major mistake in our profession. It's also another reason why I've been so cautious with both of you. You have two orbits as apprentices, there's no reason to rush. Now, Gren, if I've figured things out correctly, your sister leaves tomorrow. Is that right?"

"Yes, Sir," Gren replied.

"Then what are you doing here? You two can have the rest of the rotation off, tomorrow as well."

"Thank you, Sir," Gren said.

"Now go! I'll see you the rotation after next. Be ready to

observe, Gren, and remember, you're going to be working harder than ever."

"Thank you, Sir," Gren said. She and Lawson left the office and closed the door behind them.

"Was that really Haas?" Lawson whispered. "He's mellowed!"

"I guess one good thing came out of the mess with Thaddeus," Gren whispered back. She was aware of the fact that everyone at the office was staring at them, word of what had happened to Thaddeus had spread, but she didn't really care. She just wanted to get home and spend the last few units with her sister.

Chapter Thirty-Four

Even though they had been expecting it, the knock on the door caused everyone to jump. Gren stood up to answer. Her dwelling seemed larger than it had all break, the extra cots were gone and although the area was still small, there was suddenly room to move. Gren opened the door; Sham, Titus and Grey stood on the other side.

"Oh." Gren moved aside so they could come in.

"Gee, Gren, you certainly know how to make us feel welcome," Sham teased.

"I thought you were my parents."

Sham opened his mouth, ready to give a snappy comeback, but Titus punched him lightly on the shoulder. "We just wanted to say good-bye," Sham said instead.

"Grey, come in and sit down," Tayo suggested. He did as told. Sham and Titus continued to stand near the door.

Calli looked at her partner. "We need to get going." She gave Winnie and Mollie each as hug. Tayo followed suit. Calli hugged Lawson before approaching Gren. "I'm sorry that I…"

Gren shook her head. "Calli, don't. No regrets. It wasn't your fault, and everything turned out fine. Thank you for helping out." They embraced.

Then it was Tayo's turn. All three girls had tears in their eyes. "And to think, when we were younger we spent our breaks at home, catching up on sleep!" Tayo said, wiping her eyes.

"I miss you both so much," Gren said. "When you think about apprenticing next orbit, remember that there are a lot of practices in this area."

"We've already started putting in our applications," Calli said. She picked up her bag and took a few steps towards the door. She shook Grey's hand as she passed him, then stopped in front of Sham. "Poke."

Sham took her bag from her. "We'll walk you down."

Tayo stopped by Grey and squatted down so that she could talk to him face to face. "I just want to say…um…it was really nice getting to know you."

Grey smiled broadly. "I feel the same way. You have my address?"

Tayo nodded. "I'll write, I promise."

Grey's smile grew. "Me too. Once my leg heals, maybe I'll head up to the Learning Center sometime. Possession of Thad's glidemobile reverted to me when he was sentenced, and it's only a couple of units away."

Tayo grinned. "I'll look forward to it." She stood up and picked up her bag. "Bye." She walked towards the door. "Bye, everybody."

Calli, Tayo, Titus and Sham walked out. Even though they closed the door behind them Sham could still be heard saying, "Tayo, what is going on with you and Grey?"

Grey turned red and sunk lower into his chair.

● ○ ◐◗◑ ○ ○

A few hundreds later, there was another knock. Gren answered again. Her parents were on the other side. She was happy to see them, but sad that it meant that Winnie and Mollie were leaving. She gave each of her parents a hug and a quick kiss before they followed her inside.

"Mom, Dad!" Winnie went running into her parents' arms. "I've missed you both so much!"

Their parents said hello to everyone, and Gren introduced them to Grey.

"Did you have a good time?" their mother asked Winnie.

"It was great! Calli and Tayo took us to so many restaurants, and they let us go into the kitchens. Mollie and I met some of the greatest chefs in the area."

"What else did you do?"

"Well," Winnie said, "we spent time in the park."

"I don't really like that park," Mollie added quickly.

"Me either." Winnie and Mollie both laughed.

○ ○ ◐ ◯ ○ ○

After everyone had shared a meal, it was time for them to leave. Sham, Titus and Grey left first, giving Gren a little bit of time to say goodbye to her family in private. "Bye, kids, it's been...different," Sham said as they left.

Lawson stayed, since they considered him part of the family.

"What happened to Titus and Grey?" Gren's mother asked once they were gone. "Grey's leg...and Titus looks like he's been fighting."

"They were in a fight with Grey's brother," Winnie said quickly. It was the truth, but she didn't want her parents to know the whole story—they'd never let her visit Gren again. "He's, well, he's kind of crazy. He attacked a bunch of people. Titus and Grey were able to stop him."

"They're real heroes," Mollie added.

"His brother is in a Labor Camp now," Gren continued. "He won't be bothering anyone again." She was grateful that her own scratches and bruises had subsided enough that she could cover them with makeup.

"I hate to say this," Gren's dad started slowly, "but we need to be going. We've a long trip ahead of us."

Gren and Lawson walked everyone outside. There was another round of hugs and several more tears.

"I don't see you enough," Gren said to her mother.

"I know!" she replied. "Sometime soon, let's all take a few rotations and rent a cabin up by Lake Collins! We haven't been up there in orbits."

"Sounds like fun," Gren said, knowing that the last place she wanted to be was Lake Collins.

Gren and Lawson stood by as everyone else climbed into the glidemobile and it pulled away. Lawson put his arm around Gren. They watched long after the vehicle was out of view. Neither of them spoke, no words were necessary. When Gren was ready, she simply turned, and they walked back inside.

Epilogue

As they exited Rock 'n' Roller Coaster, Gren looked at Winnie. She was sure that her younger sister had a million questions. She had a few herself, but wasn't sure where she could get the answers. "Are you okay?"

Winnie smiled. "That was fun. Can we do it again?"

"Maybe later," Lawson said quickly. "I wouldn't mind sitting down for a few minutes, maybe grabbing something to eat."

The three of them headed to Pizza Planet without saying anything about their adventure. They ordered some food and found a table upstairs, away from everyone else.

"I've looked up a lot of information on that ride," Winnie said with a mouth full of pizza. "I've never heard it described like that before. I wonder why."

"Because your FASTPASSES are magical," a voice said behind them. They all looked to see Cassidy grabbing a chair. "Mind if I join you for a bit?" She sat down without waiting for an answer.

"Wait..." Winnie started, "...you were there!"

"Right. I'm the cast member who checked your harness before Rock 'n' Roller Coaster. That's quite a ride, especially when you're sitting in the last row. You're a very brave girl."

"That's not what I meant. You were *there*."

"Can you believe that the ride is less than two minutes long?" Cassidy asked. "It feels like so much more."

Winnie wasn't buying it. "Was that real?"

Cassidy grinned. "What is reality? Who is to say that what is happening now is really happening? Maybe this moment is just a dream."

"Don't try to confuse her anymore," Gren pleaded.

"Fair enough." Cassidy leaned close and whispered to Winnie. "It's the G-forces. They can mess with your mind."

"Don't tell me that," Winnie said. "G-forces aren't going to make me think that I was kidnapped. And they aren't going to have me make up people like Bryce or Mollie."

"It has something to do with the FASTPASSES," Lawson quickly commented. "When I rode the ride by myself without mine it was a normal ride."

"You rode it without me?" Gren teased.

"I, um..."

Gren decided to let him off the hook. "We still don't understand most of it. But when I first saw Lawson last year, I knew that I had seen him before. It wasn't even that he looked slightly familiar, I felt like we were supposed to be close friends."

"I felt the same way."

"So you've been texting nonstop ever since," Winnie added.

"Yeah, trying to figure it out. And this time, little sister, I knew that I was supposed to bring you along. I can't explain it."

"We think that maybe it's a parallel universe or something like that. For some reason we're supposed to experience it from time to time."

"So Cassidy, is that what it is?" Winnie looked around, but

Cassidy was nowhere to be seen. "Where did she go?"

"Who knows," Gren said. "Roy did the same thing to us last year."

"Was she ever really here?" Lawson added. Gren shot him a dirty look.

"Holy splarsh, Lawson, don't do that to me. I'm confused enough already."

"Winnie! You watch your language."

Winnie looked at her sister. "Why, Gren? It doesn't mean anything here, does it?"

"Well..." Gren stammered, "no. But is still doesn't sound nice."

"I have two more questions," Winnie said before taking another bite of her pizza.

"Ask us anything," Gren said. "I don't know if we'll be able to answer, but we'll try."

"Can we try Rock 'n' Roller Coaster *without* the magical FASTPASSES? I kind of want to see what the regular ride is like."

Gren smiled. "Sure, but we'll have to wait in the standby line. Next question."

"Do those magical FASTPASSES work for Tower of Terror? I've heard that ride is pretty intense as well."

"No!" Gren and Lawson immediately answered in unison.

A Mouse Gate Adventure
Book What's your adventure?
www.mousegate.com

Title: *Dream Wanderers The Escape*
- Author: Paula Brown
- Publisher: Mouse Gate Press
- Paper Back: ISBN: 9781590957912
- eBook: ISBN: 9781590958766
- Number of pages 240
- Publication Date: September, 2016

Dream Wanderers guide you through your worst night-mares.

Far across the universe, an elite school runs a special program, training the Dream Wanderers of tomorrow.

But what happens when…

Gren and Lawson will soon achieve the impossible, becoming the first male/female partners to make it through the program. Or with they? Their feelings for each other and Lawson's disdain for an unbreakable rule, risk their expulsion.

They wander into a nightmare of their own…

When Lawson and Gren disappear, most assume they've run away together. But their four best friends aren't so sure. Following a shaky clue, they enlist the help of a crazy old man and set out to find the truth. Soon, the dream Wanderers will take on an entire army, as the fate of two worlds hangs in the balance.

www.ingramcontent.com/pod-product-compliance
Lightning Source LLC
Chambersburg PA
CBHW020508120726
47904CB00003B/741